D0952926

STAR WARS

BOBA FETT™

PURSUIT

ELIZABETH HAND

LUCAS BOOKS

SCHOLASTIC INC.

New York   Toronto   London   Auckland   Sydney
Mexico City   New Delhi   Hong Kong   Buenos Aires

www.starwars.com
www.scholastic.com

ISBN 0-439-33933-2

Cover by Alicia Buelow and David Mattingly

12 11 10 9 8 7 6 5   6 7 8 9/0

Printed in the U.S.A.
First printing, December 2004

CHAPTER ONE

Death is silence: eternal, dark, colorless, without form or meaning.

Boba Fett had watched his father, Jango Fett, die, murdered by the hated Jedi Mace Windu. At the time Boba had felt only grief and rage. In the years that followed, he felt sorrow, the dull constant ache of missing his father. It was an ache that had receded somewhat over the last few years. But it had never disappeared.

The one thing Boba had never felt — had never even allowed himself to imagine — was what it would feel like to actually die. He had never believed he would experience death firsthand —

But now Boba Fett was dead.

His motionless form lay in a dark, twisting tunnel inside Mazariyan, the immense, mazelike fortress of the Separatist Tech genius Wat Tambor. Outside the citadel's walls, a fierce battle raged. The might of Wat Tambor's robotic troops was massed against the dwindling resources of the Republic, led by the Jedi General Glynn-Beti. The walls of Mazariyan shuddered beneath repeated bombardments by the Republic troops. Fissures appeared in the floor, only to be immediately repaired by microscopic nanotechs. A crack ran across the ceiling above Boba's lifeless body. A thick, mucuslike substance began to drip down — the organically derived fluid used to power Wat Tambor's massive array of machines.

Had Boba been alive, he would have known this was a bad sign. The Republic had breached the outermost of Mazariyan's defenses. The living fortress had been so badly damaged that it was losing the ability to repair itself quickly enough to survive the Republic's assault.

But Boba knew nothing of this. Boba was dead — or so it seemed. Just millimeters from his cold hand lay a small clump of pale xabar fungus. The fungus produced a paralyzing toxin. The toxin's effect was, fortunately, not permanent. To all appearances, someone under its influence appeared to be dead. Boba had grabbed the fungus in a last-ditch effort to save himself from a fatal encounter with the terrible Grievous, a partial droid general in the Separatist army.

But now it seemed that Boba's desperate effort might have failed. . . .

CHAPTER TWO

"There it is." A flat, affectless voice rang through the dark passage. "The infiltrator's corpse."

"Excellent." A second voice echoed in the empty tunnel. "Human carrion. We shouldn't waste our resources on it. It is of no use to us. We should leave it to rot."

"That would be against orders. Wat Tambor said it is to be incinerated. There must be no evidence that it was ever here."

Two spindly figures rounded the tunnel and began to approach Boba's motionless body — a pair of PK-4 worker droids. These were not battle droids — Wat Tambor had commandeered all of those to defend Mazariyan. Only a skeletal force of worker and repair droids remained inside.

But even they would be leaving soon. . . .

KKKKAAARROOOOOW!

The worker droids paused as the entire fortress

shook. The crack in the ceiling yawned wider. More of the thick, cold fluid oozed down onto Boba's helmet. It seeped beneath the edge of the visor, dripping onto his skin. Its touch was cold, icy cold, spreading like frigid fingers across Boba's cheek.

For the first time since he had been left for dead, Boba felt something.

Father?

Deep within Boba's mind, a spark of consciousness flickered. He could neither move nor speak.

But he could feel. Sensation was slowly returning to his inert form. Another blast shook Wat Tambor's fortress. Protoplasmic gunk surged from where the ceiling had been blown apart. As the PK-4s stood, waiting for the blast to subside, more of the icy ooze dripped upon Boba's gloved hand. Some of it covered the bare patch of skin that he had deliberately exposed to the xabar fungus.

And now, that icy touch set off a chain reaction within Boba's brain.

Memory flared through him. He could not blink, or speak — but he could remember. The chill touch of organic ooze became the touch of Jango's hand upon his cheek. As though awakening from a dream, he remembered his father's face. Then the dream grew nightmarish as he remembered his father's death. He moaned.

Memory was returning to Boba Fett.

Memory, and consciousness —

And life!

Mazariyan, he thought groggily. *The battle . . . Grievous . . . Wat Tambor . . .*

"We must hurry." The droids stood above Boba's body. He quickly stifled his groan as one droid prodded him. Its insectile head swiveled to stare at the bounty hunter. "Wat Tambor wants no evidence that a spy gained entry."

The entire fortress shook once more.

"Another blast! No time to waste!" The second droid bent. Its servogrip hands slid roughly beneath Boba's arms.

Agggghhhhhh! Boba wanted to gasp with pain. As memory flooded him, so did further sensation — primarily pain. Grievous's last blow had penetrated Boba's body armor. He could feel where the armor had shattered upon impact, exposing his shoulder to the energy bolt.

The blow had not been fatal. But the pain was excruciating. Fortunately, he had not cried out. The droids still thought he was dead.

Far from it! Boba could feel his lungs expanding

as he took in air. He could feel the droids' servo-grips tightening around him. He was tall and muscular, and his body armor added to his bulk.

But the droids hoisted him up between them effortlessly, roughly — as though he was nothing but a sack of refuse. Or fuel for Wat Tambor's furnace . . .

Which, to them, he was.

Agh, he thought, gritting his teeth. He could *definitely* feel pain.

And he could see.

"The incinerator has been busy today," one of the droids commented as they began to stride quickly down the tunnel. "Much organic matter to feed on."

"Human scum," the second droid retorted. They stumbled as another blast rocked the fortress.

Boba blinked. *Good thing I've still got my helmet on*, he thought. *Otherwise they might notice my eyes are open.*

He tried to find his bearings as the droids bore him down, down, down through a series of long, twisting passages. Glowing lumens showed where the fortress walls had sustained considerable damage from the Republic's assault. Shattered droids were everywhere, as well as glowing heaps of molten metal.

Wonder who has the upper hand now? Boba thought. He hated the Jedi, but General Glynn-Beti had helped him gain entry into Mazariyan. The last Boba had seen of the battle, the Republic's troops were putting up a good fight against the Separatists. If Wat Tambor's forces had been weakened by the battle, it would be that much easier for Boba to escape and find his way back to his ship, *Slave I*.

But first he had to avoid being tossed into Wat Tambor's furnace!

He took a chance and flexed one of his hands. His strength was returning. As it did, the pain from Grievous's blast began to subside.

My body armor must've absorbed most of the blow, Boba thought gratefully. He could feel himself growing stronger, more alert. It was a real effort not to move and strike out at the droids.

But while sensation was slowly returning to his body, he still felt slightly groggy. His reflexes would not be as keen as they should be.

And he had no idea who, or what, he might encounter inside the fortress.

Better wait . . . he thought.

"This way," one of the droids announced. Boba did his best not to flinch as they made a sudden turn and began to descend down a steep incline.

The darkness took on an unmistakable reddish tinge. Inside his Mandalorian body armor, Boba started to sweat.

The good news is that I've recovered enough from that fungus to feel the heat, he thought with grim amusement. *And the bad news? This must be the incinerator!*

Around him, everything glowed as though it were molten. The droids' shining silver limbs burned crimson and gold. The heat was intense and painful. A slight adjustment of his body armor's thermostatic cooling system would take care of that, but Boba didn't dare move to change it.

Not yet, anyway. He turned his head ever so slightly, praying that his helmet would hide any apparent motion from his droid captors. They seemed to take no notice.

"Wat Tambor will be departing shortly," one of the droids stated in its flat voice. "He wished to be informed when the spy was disposed of."

"Disposal is imminent," the other droid replied.

Boba stared through his helmet's visor as the droids carried him the last few steps to their destination. They were in a large, nearly airless room, devoid of any equipment or furnishings. A few meters away shone an incandescent square of light, blinding and seemingly as hot as the sun. Heat radiated from it in shimmering waves. A conveyor belt, the room's sole machinery, moved slowly toward the incinerator's opening.

Talk about too hot to handle, thought Boba. Sweat trickled down his face, stinging his eyes. He couldn't move to wipe it away. Beneath him, the droids stopped. Their servogrips remained in place, holding Boba above their heads. He took a deep breath, then tightened his muscles until his body went taut.

Have to risk it — hope they don't notice!

The droids remained oblivious. In front of them the conveyor belt moved slowly, steadily, toward the incinerator.

And now Boba could see other shapes on it. Mangled knots of metal and plasteel, all that remained of damaged droids, and — shocking Boba — lifeless bundles of body armor, flesh, and charred weaponry.

Clones, he thought, and felt a stab of mingled pity and horror. Helmets covered their faces, but Boba knew what he would see if their body armor was removed —

His father Jango's face. His own face . . . for Jango had been the template from which all the clones had been built. Including Boba, the only un-altered clone.

"Shall we retain its armor and helmet?" One of the droids asked as it hoisted Boba. Its servogrip tugged at his weapons belt. "These are not organic. They are of fine quality."

You bet they are! Boba gritted his teeth. It took every bit of willpower to keep from lunging at the droids now; but their hold on him was still too strong. *Gotta wait till the last possible moment . . .*

"Our orders were to dispose of it completely," the second droid stated. "It is time we returned and gave our report."

The first droid's servogrip retracted. Boba allowed himself a silent sigh of relief. He felt himself being lifted higher, until he was poised directly above the conveyor belt. The incinerator's mouth was close enough that he could feel its heat through his reinforced boots. He stared down and watched as the conveyor brought one of the lifeless clones to the furnace's opening. For an instant the gray-clad form seemed to hang in the air, silhouetted black against white-gold flames. There was a flare of scarlet, a thread of black smoke — and it was gone.

Nothing can withstand that heat! Boba took a

deep breath. The air was so hot it was like inhaling molten lava.

Boba thought of all the things he hadn't done yet. The vows he had made: to become the greatest bounty hunter the galaxy had ever known, and to seek revenge on the Jedi who had killed Jango Fett.

He vowed once more to see these things through.

"Ready," one of the droids said.

"Ready," agreed its partner. Without a sound, they flung Boba toward the belt.

For a moment he hung in the air, limp as the dead things beneath him. Then with a wordless shout Boba straightened, launching himself toward the droids. With a satisfying *thunk!* his boots connected with the droids' heads. They went sprawling, and Boba landed behind them before they could recover.

Good thing these worker droids are unarmed.

"Alert Wat Tambor!" one of them commanded. Its insectoid photoreceptors flashed from green to red as they surveyed Boba. "There has been a breach on Level Three. Organic matter has reanimated. Request backup immedi —"

"That's your last request!" Boba yelled.

He drew his blaster, staggering slightly. *Still un-*

steady from that toxin! He caught himself, leveling a charge that sent the first droid reeling backward onto the moving belt. The second swiveled. It, too, was unarmed, but Boba could hear a blast of static as it attempted to send an alarm signal from its vocabulator.

"Things sure are heating up around here!" Boba kicked out at the second droid. It collapsed against the side of the conveyor. Before it could move again, Boba blasted it. Remnants of plasteel and sensors rained down onto the conveyor belt, as the first droid was borne into the furnace. "I think it's time I checked out —"

He shoved his blaster back into his belt and turned. Behind him was an opening.

That must be how I got here. A shrill alarm sounded. *And it looks like it's how I better leave — now!*

He ran through the opening into a narrow passage. Muted thunder came from outside. The floor beneath him shook. Boba looked around but saw no signs of life anywhere; only piles of rubble where the Republic's fire had damaged the fortress walls. The passage went in only one direction, so he began to run swiftly, one gloved hand resting lightly on his blaster.

I've got to find Wat Tambor, he thought with grim determination. *If he gets away . . .*

Boba quickly pushed that thought aside. He had been sent to Xagobah to capture Wat Tambor and bring him back to Jabba the Hutt, dead or alive.

Failure was not an option.

CHAPTER THREE

Boba had no idea how to find his way out of Wat Tambor's fortress, let alone find the Foreman of the Separatist's Techno Union before he fled Xagobah. He continued to follow the passage as it twisted and turned, gradually climbing toward one of Mazariyan's upper levels. Welcome cool air flowed past him, and Boba inhaled gratefully.

You never know how much you miss breathing till you've been dead, he thought wryly.

He came to a spot where the tunnel forked. Here he paused. It was easier to breathe now; easier to do everything. The xabar's toxins had finally worn off.

But Boba couldn't blame everything on the toxin. He inspected his body armor and noted where it had been damaged by Grievous's assault. As he ran a hand over his arm he winced.

That was a bad one, he thought. A surface wound;

but Grievous's weaponry and lightsabers had managed to tear right through the Mandalorian body armor. *Better make sure I treat th —*

KARAM!

With a cry Boba fell backward. Blinding heat surrounded him. With one hand he gripped his blaster, moving carefully to see what had happened.

One entire side of the fortress was gone. Where moments before the tunnel's wall had curved, now there was only empty air, a scorched ring of rock and metal, and the slimy, organic mass Wat Tambor had bioengineered from Xagobah's native fungi. Warily, Boba approached the opening and peered out.

Below, all was chaos. The main entrance to Mazariyan had been breached. Clone troopers stormed through a huge gaping hole, tendrils of smoke still rising from its edges.

"Whoa," Boba said in grudging admiration. "That was the explosion I felt back there in the tunnel! The Republic must've used a thermal detonator to blow their way in. Man, I'd love to get my hands on one of those. . . ."

He stared down to where clone troopers ran between the fortress and an AT-TE — a Republic all-terrain–tactical-enforcer. A pall of smoke hung above the ground, mingling with the purplish spores that pervaded Xagobah's atmosphere. At the edge of the clearing that surrounded Mazariyan, blasted malvil-trees oozed and burned. Flames licked up from the ruins of an immense hailfire droid. There were blasted spider droids and battle droids. The charred remnants of a Fromm tower droid were scattered across the ground like the ruins of a small city. A few beleaguered battle droids still made their way across the battlefield, firing relentlessly as the clones rushed toward and past them.

It was clear that the Republic now had the upper hand.

"Wat Tambor must have given the signal to retreat," Boba muttered. "He came here to regroup after he escaped from the Republic. Now that Glynn-Beti's tracked him to his lair, he's got no reason to stick around."

Boba craned his neck to look into the sky. Sure enough, airspeeders and even a few Jedi starfighters crisscrossed the violet haze, as though searching for someone.

Wat Tambor, thought Boba. *And they better not find him before I do!*

A sudden blast of laser fire ricocheted from the

ruined wall beside him. Boba ducked back inside the gaping hole.

"That was way too close." He peered out. Far below, a clone trooper was pointing up to where Boba had stood just seconds ago. Before the trooper could alert others to his presence, Boba whipped out his weapon and sent a return blast flaring through the smoke. The clone trooper fell, a blackened hole where his chest had been.

"Time to get back to *Slave I*," Boba said. He reached back to touch a small squarish object mounted near his weapons belt. As a matter of caution, he'd left his primary jet pack back on the ship. But he still had his liquid-cable launcher.

Good thing, too. It's a long, long way down.

He stepped cautiously out onto the edge of the blasted wall. Below, the Republic's troops continued to mill about the battleground. But most of the clones now seemed to be leaving the fortress, heading back to their troop carriers. Boba shaded his eyes, adjusting his helmet so that he could better focus through the smoke and spore-haze.

"There." His gloved hand stabbed at the air. "That's Glynn-Beti's airspeeder . . ."

He watched as the Jedi general drew her craft closer to the AT-TE at the clearing's edge. Glynn-

Beti had helped him earlier on Xagobah, after Boba had saved her reckless young apprentice, Ulu Ulix, from certain death.

But Boba knew better than to expect any mercy from her now. And the mere thought of the Jedi made Boba's gut tighten with anger.

That Jedi scum Mace Windu murdered my father, he thought. He glanced back at the corpse of the clone trooper he'd killed in self-defense minutes ago. The clone's helmet had rolled away from his slack face.

Jango Fett's face.

Boba's expression grew grim. He stared back at the AT-TE. The diminutive figure of General Glynn-Beti had dismounted from the airspeeder and was now approaching the vehicle.

"She'll be giving orders to her crew," Boba said. "Now's my chance. . . ."

Raising his arms slightly, he leaped from the fortress wall and launched the liquid-cable, which hooked to a faraway tree. The ground rushed toward him. He could smell burning metal and the stink of charred fungus. Wind and smoke flashed past him as Boba Fett swung above the battlefield, heading toward the forest that hid his ship — and freedom!

CHAPTER FOUR

"There!" From the ground far below Boba, came a sudden shout. "A spy! Fire on him!"

Boba twisted to look down. A knot of clone troopers was running from the AT-TE, pointing up at him as they drew their weapons.

This secondary jet pack's only good for a short sprint. Can't waste time firing on them! Boba thought with regret. He yanked his jet pack's thruster to full force and tore through the air, blaster fire echoing at his heels. Just a few yards ahead of him was the forest of immense mushroomlike trees. *Now if I can just get undercover —*

A blaze of laser fire ripped through the trees closest to him. Debris and fungal ooze rained down on Boba as he steered his way beneath the canopy. As the violet shadows closed around him, he grabbed his own blaster and turned, sending a sudden volley back toward the ground. Two of the clone troopers fell. The other raced toward the forest, only to stop abruptly as a clear voice echoed from the AT-TE.

"Hold your fire!"

Boba grabbed hold of a malvil-tree branch and swung himself onto it, catching his breath. He looked down and saw the clones returning to the AT-TE. A small uniformed figure stared back at the forest. Even at this distance, Boba could feel the force of Glynn-Beti's piercing gaze upon him. He stared back, bold and unafraid, then turned and used the jet pack to bring himself back down to ground level.

"Just in time," he said as he touched down. He heard the familiar droning sound of the auxiliary jet pack's fuel cell expiring. He shut it off, keeping his hand on his blaster, and began to run. His shoulder ached from Grievous's wound, but he ignored the pain.

Got to get airborne before Wat Tambor does. . . .

The forest was a tangled mass of fungus and ropy vines. Boba made his way carefully through the trees, his weapon at the ready. Now and then he glanced over his shoulder for signs of pursuit.

But he saw no one. *There must be a mass exodus from this place*, he thought. *The Republic and*

Separatists alike. That means Xagobah will finally be given back to the Xamsters. . . .

Boba felt a small pulse of relief, recalling the natives of Xagobah who had helped him when he first arrived on-planet. The gentle Xamsters had suffered under Wat Tambor's reign, either killed outright or forced to fight against the Republic. Now, at last, they would be free again.

After a few minutes Boba's steps slowed. Around him the malvil-trees grew thickly, undamaged by warfare. Somewhere, behind these huge mushroom-like plants, *Slave I* waited, hidden by its cloaking device.

Boba stopped, listening for any sounds of pursuit.

Nothing. He touched the sensor on his weapons belt, deactivating the cloaking device. There was a low hum. Then the sleek outlines of his starship took shape in the small clearing in front of him. Boba allowed himself a rare smile.

"Good to see you again," he murmured.

He walked slowly around *Slave I*, inspecting the ship for any signs of damage. But *Slave I* had weathered its time on Xagobah better than Boba had. He checked the missile launcher under its concealed panel and made sure the blaster cannons hadn't been affected by Xagobah's humid atmosphere. Then, with a quick look around to make sure he was unobserved, he boarded his ship.

Inside, everything was as he had left it. He took off his helmet and set it alongside the control console. Then he grabbed a medpac and slapped a dermibandage onto his wounded shoulder. The repairs to his body armor would have to wait. He slid into the cockpit console and prepared for departure. As *Slave I*'s motors hummed to life, Boba did a fast scan of his tracking computer. A set of coordinates flashed onto the screen, along with the image of a *Hardcell*-class interstellar transport —

Wat Tambor's ship.

"Gotcha!" Boba cried in triumph. More information scrolled across his monitor.

VESSEL REGISTERED WITH TECHNO UNION. VESSEL DEPARTURE IMMINENT.

"Time to go," said Boba. He programmed *Slave I*'s tracking device to monitor Tambor's ship, then hit the thrusters. Like an arrow loosed from a taut bow, *Slave I* shot into the air. Xagobah's murky atmosphere surrounded the ship, but the flickering image of Wat Tambor's vessel shone clearly from the computer screen. Within moments, *Slave I* had cleared the atmosphere and entered the familiar star-shot darkness of space.

Behind the control console, Boba stared determinedly out at the expanse of stars. He observed the stationary mass of the Republic's troopship, and a single flare of light like a beacon: Wat Tambor's ship.

"Don't bother trying to run," he said as *Slave I* shot off in pursuit of the craft. "No escape for you."

Wat Tambor's ship was designed for interstellar transport, not fighting. That gave Boba the advantage — or so he thought. He got the Techno Union foreman's vessel in his sights, bringing *Slave I* as close as he dared before firing.

BLAAAAAMMM!

One of Boba's laser cannons released its payload: two large blasts of compressed atomic energy.

"Sorry, Jabba," Boba crowed. "You said 'dead or alive,' but it looks like you're gonna have to settle for dead. . . ."

He angled *Slave I* to the side, hoping for a better

view of Wat Tambor's destruction. But the wily foreman hadn't spent all those years with the Techno Union for nothing. As Boba stared in dismay, a shimmering deflector shield seemed to swallow Tambor's ship like a vast cloud. At the same time, a sleekly shining concussion missile streaked from the transport. A moment later, a second missile followed. The first missile's homing sensor sent it racing toward Boba's energy bolt. There was a blinding flash as it impacted, and Boba muttered under his breath. Concussive waves rippled through the depths of space. *Slave I* shuddered.

But Boba wasted no time on anger or regret. The second missile's tracking sensors had locked into *Slave I* — the missile was heading right toward him. *Slave I* shot up and sideways. The missile swerved and followed. Before it could strike its target, Boba loosed a volley from his blaster cannons.

"How 'bout this, Tambor?" he challenged.

He heard the satisfying *thnnk* of impact. Nanoseconds later, the missile imploded.

But there was more enemy fire coming! Boba withdrew *Slave I* to a better firing range, then blasted the enemy vessel.

"If I can just weaken his deflector shield," said

Boba, his console tilting forward as he took aim and fired. "Then go in for the kill!"

Pinwheels of energy flared and pulsed around Wat Tambor's ship. Retaliatory blasts echoed around *Slave I*, but Boba was too fast —

KARRAAM!

A jaw-rattling blast as Wat Tambor scored a hit, penetrating Boba's shield defenses. He glanced quickly at the monitor, saw nothing serious. His face tightened with fury as *Slave I* soared toward the enemy ship. He waited until the last possible moment, then fired.

BLAM!

A hit! Boba whooped as Wat Tambor's vessel rocked dangerously. He'd breached the defense shield! Boba's hand hovered above the console panel. Another moment and he'd have a clear shot — and Wat Tambor would be his!

Tatooine, here I come!

At that moment, something streaked into view. Another vessel, whipping past Wat Tambor's ship like a ghostly flame. Boba sucked his breath in sharply.

I know that ship!

He'd heard about it on Tatooine, listening to the

other bounty hunters recount firefights and acts of cold savagery directed against the Jedi.

Asajj Ventress, Boba thought. He watched as her starship swooped closer.

Asajj! She might have been the only other person in the galaxy who hated the Jedi as much as he did. Raised on the hostile, rapacious world of Rattatak, Asajj had been trained by a young Jedi marooned on her terrible planet. Ky Narec had been not only stranded on Rattatak — he had been effectively abandoned by his Masters, who had never sought to aid the young Jedi — or his protégé, Asajj, who longed to escape her cruel homeworld.

But the Jedi never came. Asajj never had the chance to prove herself to them, or to anyone but her mentor. And when Ky Narec died, Asajj vowed to avenge herself upon the Jedi. Allying herself with Count Dooku, Asajj had become one of the Republic's fiercest and most deadly opponents. Her control of the Force was exceptional, but her rage was overwhelming, as were her combat skills . . . and her prowess with a starship. Boba watched with ungrudging admiration as Asajj's vessel cleaved through space.

What an ally she would be! he thought. *We could take on Mace Windu together.*

No. Boba shook his head.

Mace Windu is mine alone, he thought, feeling a spike of rage. *No one will deny me vengeance. No one . . .*

A barrage of blasts shattered his thoughts. Barely a klick away, Asajj Ventress's ship was hurtling right toward *Slave I.*

She thinks I'm part of the Republic force! Slave I shot upward as Boba outmaneuvered Asajj. *If only she knew the truth!*

But the truth would be wasted on Asajj Ventress. She was here as part of Wat Tambor's backup force. And at this moment, she knew only one thing:

An unknown ship was firing on the Techno Union foreman.

And whoever piloted that spacecraft was going to die.

CHAPTER FIVE

BRRAAAK!

A deafening roar from Asajj Ventress's ion cannons shook *Slave I*. Frantically, Boba fired back at Ventress's ship.

But she was far too fast. As he watched, her ship vaulted over *Slave I*. Before he could fire back, Ventress's laser cannons released a barrage of energy blasts.

BAM!

A direct hit!

Boba was nearly jolted from his console. He sent a rain of return fire, but it was too late. *Slave I* vibrated furiously as a second plasma blast hit home.

Gotta get away, Boba thought grimly. *Can't lose Wat Tambor. . . .*

Slave I shot after the Separatist's vessel.

And Asajj Ventress shot after *Slave I*. Boba piloted his ship up, angling until Asajj was directly below him. He checked that *Slave I*'s mines were primed, then sent an ion mine whirling toward her.

BLAM!

"Yes!"

But immediately Boba's yelp of triumph turned to disappointment, as the mine ricocheted harmlessly from Ventress's defense field, to spin off into space. At the same moment, a burst of retaliatory ion fire blazed from Asajj's cannons.

BRAAK!

Boba groaned as *Slave I* rocked sharply to starboard. He fired back, but once more Asajj was too quick. He let the ship veer to one side, hoping to buy a few precious seconds as he checked the damage.

A glance at *Slave I*'s repair files gave him the bad news. Some of the outer panels had been loosened. Serious damage, but not fatal.

The starboard wing was another story. Two of the fins shielding the repulsor grilles had been destroyed. Without them, *Slave I* was crippled — he could fly, but his nav skills were seriously impaired. Worse, landing the ship would be a real problem —

Not that he could even think about landing now!

BAM!

Another hit for Asajj. Boba fired off two missiles,

had the satisfaction of seeing one rip into the side of her starfighter. A starburst of plasma glowed gold and white, then faded.

"No." Boba scowled. Asajj's defense shields had absorbed the blow. And Wat Tambor's transport remained unscathed.

"Time for a new tactic," Boba muttered.

He punched a series of commands into his console. A grid popped onto a monitor, displaying the coordinates of an asteroid belt not far off. If he could lure Asajj there, he might have a better chance of losing her. Then he could make a swift pass back toward Wat Tambor. . . .

He set *Slave I*'s thrusters to maximum. The ship veered toward the asteroid field.

And right into Asajj Ventress's line of fire!

Boba retaliated, trying to dodge Ventress's attack. But the damage done to *Slave I*'s starboard wing slowed him too much. As he made one last-ditch attempt to fire, a flaming burst from Ventress's ion cannon blazed toward him. Desperately, Boba tried to avoid the blast.

BLLAAAAMM!

With a cry Boba yanked at the thruster. But it was no good.

Slave I was finished.

CHAPTER SIX

With a screaming roar, Boba's ship fell into a nosedive. He hit the backup thrusters, momentarily righting *Slave I*, then looked up.

He expected to see Asajj's ship looming before him — or, worse, another blinding blast from her ion cannons.

What he didn't expect to see was a Jedi starfighter.

"Whoa!" Boba let out a gasp of disbelief. "That's Anakin Skywalker!"

He had seen the legendary Jedi apprentice twice now, both times from a distance. Most recently, Boba had watched as Skywalker successfully destroyed a Separatist ramship on Xagobah. Skywalker's combat skill was as keen as his defiance — and both were attributes Boba admired.

"He's driving off Ventress!" Boba said in disbelief.

Skywalker's starfighter took after Asajj's ship like a winged tumnor attacking its prey. As Boba watched, the young Jedi fired a volley of precision blasts, each one finding its target — Asajj Ventress!

The battle was over almost as quickly as it had begun. Asajj's starship raced away from Skywalker. Boba shook his head in admiration and faint disappointment.

She hardly put up a fight at all!

He craned his neck, following her — and saw why she'd fled so quickly.

Wat Tambor's transport vessel was glowing, radiant white as though consumed by a sun's heat. Boba only had time to groan, as the transport seemed to billow and burst . . .

And made the jump into hyperspace.

It was all a diversion! Boba fumed, furious at himself. *Asajj wanted to distract me so that Wat Tambor could escape —*

"And she succeeded!" he said angrily. "How could I have been so stupid? Well, it'll never happen again. . . ."

He'd be sure of that! Boba might make mistakes — but he never made the same one twice.

Especially not with Jabba the Hutt wanting results.

Boba's expression grew somber at the thought of the notorious gangster. Wat Tambor could be anywhere in the galaxy by now. Boba had no way of knowing where. And, with *Slave I* damaged, no way of following —

"IDENTIFY YOURSELF!"

Boba started as a crackle of static came through *Slave I*'s speakers.

"IDENTIFY YOURSELF OR BE DESTROYED!"

Boba stabbed at the console panel. "Identify *your*self!" he countered.

"ANAKIN SKYWALKER, OF THE REPUBLIC'S XAGOBAH PEACEKEEPING FORCE. I HAVE ORDERS TO DESTROY ALL SEPARATIST VESSELS WITHIN THIS AIRSPACE. YOU HAVE TEN SECONDS TO IDENTIFY YOURSELF OR RISK DESTRUCTION. TEN. NINE. . . ."

Gotta stall! Boba thought. Identifying himself as a mercenary bounty hunter wouldn't go over too well with Skywalker.

But the young Jedi was part of the Republic force that had driven Wat Tambor from Xagobah. Maybe he would have some idea as to where the Techno Union foreman had fled — information that

Boba could use to track Wat Tambor down himself, and still claim Jabba's bounty . . .

". . . FOUR. THREE. . . ."

I better be fast, thought Boba. *And I better be good!*

"Skywalker — this is a request for assistance!" he announced into the comm unit. Boba knew this was the Jedi's weak spot — they could never resist being the good guys. "My ship was damaged in a firefight with Asajj Ventress — repeat, request assistance immediately. . . ."

Silence. In front of him, Anakin's starship hovered like a silver flame. As he spoke, Boba punched in a set of coordinates. A navscreen flickered to life — and there was the information Boba needed.

Just beyond the asteroid belt, a small moon orbited Xagobah. *If I can get there, I can repair the starboard wing. And once I lose this Jedi, I can get back on Wat Tambor's trail. . . .*

Anakin's voice once more boomed through the comm unit.

"WE HAVE NO RECORD OF A SEPARATIST VESSEL FITTING YOUR DESCRIPTION," he announced. He almost sounded disappointed. "NOR DO WE HAVE RECORDS INDICATING YOU ARE PART OF THE REPUBLIC'S PEACEKEEPING FORCE —"

"I fought on the side of the Xamsters," Boba broke in quickly. That was true enough. "And now I'm heading for that moon to make repairs. So —"

Keeping a close watch on the Jedi starfighter, Boba began to slowly bank *Slave I* toward the moon.

"— if you'll just let me go, I can get my job done — and so can you."

Boba knew he was taking a risk. There was no way he could outfly Skywalker now, not with *Slave I*'s shattered wing — though once that was repaired, he'd give him a run for his credits!

Plus, Skywalker must have better things to do than waste time with an injured mercenary! thought Boba. Then he looked up.

Hmmm. Apparently not — Anakin's streamlined starfighter filled *Slave I*'s viewscreen.

"MY SHIP WILL ESCORT YOU," Anakin said. He made the simple statement sound like an order. "IF YOU CHANGE COURSE, YOUR SHIP WILL BE DESTROYED."

"I'll try not to forget that," Boba snapped — after he'd switched off the comm unit.

He reset *Slave I*'s coordinates and headed for the moon. It looked barren and uninhabited, its surface pocked with craters. The atmosphere was thin, but it would sustain human life-forms — for a little while, anyway.

Boba intended to be there only a short time. He scoped out a narrow valley between two craters and prepared *Slave I* for landing. Skywalker's ship trailed him, close enough that Boba couldn't have eluded him if he'd tried.

Somehow, that didn't seem like a good idea at the moment.

Boba throttled down, and *Slave I* began its final descent. Boba watched impassively as Skywalker's ship followed him like a shining shadow. Within minutes *Slave I* had touched down. Seconds later the starfighter did the same.

"STAY WHERE YOU ARE," a voice crackled through the base comm unit.

Boba snorted. No way he was going to stay here like a placid Khommite strider, just waiting to be picked off! He checked his weapons belt, making sure his blasters were well-concealed. Then he grabbed his helmet and started for the door.

And stopped.

Boba's Mandalorian battle helmet had belonged to his father, Jango Fett, before he was killed by Mace Windu. For the last few years Boba had worn it, along with his father's body armor. Even after all this time, Boba missed his father terribly; the armor was one of the few legacies Jango had left to his son. Boba wore it with pride and skill. Jango's helmet and armor had become a dreaded sight to all whom Boba hunted down.

But did Boba want to be recognized right now?

For a moment he brooded. He was here now because a high-ranking member of the Republic had paid off Jabba, requesting that the Huttese gangster have one of his bounty hunters track down and kill Wat Tambor. The Republic wanted Wat Tambor's death to appear to be the work of a lone assassin. And Jabba had known that only his best bounty hunter — Boba Fett — would be able to kill the wily Techno Union foreman.

But Boba had failed. So far, anyway.

Anakin Skywalker was leading Republic troops in their continuing strife with the Separatists. What if he knew of Boba's mission? If word got back to Jabba the Hutt, Boba's reputation would be ruined!

More than his reputation — his life.

And I have kind of a sentimental attachment to that, Boba thought.

He looked at the Mandalorian helmet, then glanced out the viewscreen. Anakin Skywalker was clambering down from his starfighter. Puffs of sand rose as his booted feet made contact with the moon's surface. He paused to give his starfighter a cursory damage inspection, then turned and headed for *Slave I*.

Boba took a deep breath. Reluctantly he removed his helmet — for now.

"This is only temporary," he said, catching a glimpse of himself in the dark viewscreen. He looked grim and determined, a younger, rangier version of his father. The superficial resemblance he bore to Jango Fett's clones had long since been etched away by strife and battle. A clone didn't survive long enough to wear his experiences upon his face.

But years of hunting and killing had hardened Boba's expression. He smiled seldom these days. When he did, it was usually when he saw his friend Ygabba and her father, Gab'borah, back on Tatooine.

But he wasn't on Tatooine now. And he wasn't going to return there until he could report Wat Tambor's death or capture to Jabba the Hutt.

Inside the ship, a low, warning note signaled the arrival of an intruder. The young bounty hunter disengaged the alarm, then opened the exit bay.

One hand resting lightly upon his weapons belt, the other poised above his blaster, Boba Fett strode out to meet Anakin Skywalker.

CHAPTER SEVEN

The surface of the moon was chill and stark — nearly as cold and relentless as the gaze of the young man who awaited Boba Fett. As the bounty hunter descended, he sized up the Jedi. Like Boba, much of Anakin Skywalker's youthfulness had been burned away by combat and hardship. He was taller than Boba, clad in a young Jedi's distinctive tunic, modified to suit his tastes, and knee-high boots, with unkempt hair down to his shoulders. He had a Jedi's bearing and discipline, a Jedi's skill, and a Jedi's lightsaber at his side.

But the arrogance that Boba saw in Anakin's eyes was not the mark of a Jedi. Nor was Anakin's impatience. Boba kept his own dark eyes alert and mistrustful, and left one hand on his blaster as he walked down from his craft.

The two were well-matched. Boba was strong and powerfully built, if lacking somewhat in Anakin's agility. Nor did the young bounty hunter have the Jedi's extreme pride. Pride took energy — energy better invested in concentration and cunning. In this matter, at least, Boba had the upper hand.

"That was good flying you did back there," Boba said. His expression remained aloof, but he inclined his head slightly, acknowledging Anakin's skill. "You probably saved me."

Anakin looked slightly taken aback. But he recovered quickly.

"'Probably'?" he asked, raising an eyebrow. "More like *definitely*." He looked past Boba to *Slave I*'s starboard wing. "You took quite a hit," he said, then added grudgingly, "but you put up a good fight, too. Asajj is a deadly enemy. Not many have survived an encounter with her. You were lucky — Boba Fett."

Now it was Boba's turn to look surprised. His body tensed instinctively, ready to spring into action if he had to.

But Anakin only continued to regard him with the same cool, appraising gaze. "Yes. I know who you are — and have for a long time. My Master, Obi-Wan Kenobi, has spoken of you."

Boba felt his stomach clench. Obi-Wan Kenobi! Boba and his father had escaped from the hated

Jedi back on their homeworld, Kamino. Could Kenobi have been the one to order Wat Tambor's assassination?

Boba looked warily at Anakin. He half-expected to hear the young Jedi speak of Boba's failure to capture the Separatist mastermind.

Instead, Anakin was looking at Boba thoughtfully, as though he were a chess piece on a playing board.

"Yes, I have heard of you," Anakin went on at last. "And I have seen you, as well — back there on Xagobah, when you saved Glynn-Beti's apprentice. That was brave. And reckless." The slightest smile tugged at Anakin's mouth, and he released his hold on his lightsaber. "Nice work."

"Thanks." Boba felt himself relax a little. He turned, glancing under *Slave I* to see what damage there was that he had missed.

"It mostly seems to be the wing," said Anakin. He strode past Boba and crouched to inspect it more closely. "See here? Looks like the struts were weakened to begin with. And this —"

Boba watched, amused, as Anakin crawled under his ship. The Jedi pulled a small toolkit from his tunic.

"— this really should have been taken care of a

long time ago. How long has it been since you've had this ship serviced?"

Boba shrugged. He thought of Qinx, his mechanic back on Tatooine, and Boba's longstanding request to have *Slave I*'s shield upgraded and his exterior weapons systems overhauled. "Too long, probably," he answered.

"That's for sure." Anakin shook his head. He ran his hand along one of the ship's thruster nozzles. "You've done a lot of the work on this yourself, haven't you?"

"I've made some improvements."

"Quite a few, it looks like." Anakin flashed Boba a rare look of admiration. "This is good work. It's a good ship. And you're lucky the damage wasn't worse. I can probably get this wing straightened out without too much trouble."

Anakin hesitated. Probably wondering what Obi-Wan would say of this.

A Jedi should never let down his guard, Boba answered in his head. *A Jedi's loyalty is to the Order first, then to the Republic. . . .*

Abruptly, Anakin's keen blue gaze fixed on Boba. "Don't try anything, Fett. I've got full backup from Glynn-Beti." Anakin ran a hand along his lightsaber. "Not that I'd need her help."

Boba ignored the implied threat. "I've got work to do myself," he said roughly. Grimacing, he touched his wounded shoulder.

"You better take care of that," said Anakin before turning his attention back to *Slave I*.

"And my body armor," said Boba, more to himself than the Jedi. He started back up the gangway to his ship. Suddenly he halted, frowning. "Did you hear that?"

"Huh?" Anakin's muffled voice drifted from behind the starboard wing.

Boba stood on alert, listening. His keen eyes took in the barren moonscape: pale reddish sand carved into funnels and outcroppings like ruined towers or the remains of other, wasted spacecraft. Between large craters, smaller tunnels yawned, black as the star-scattered sky beyond.

But there was no sign of life. No one but Boba Fett and Anakin Skywalker moved in this desolate place.

"Nothing," Boba said. "Must've just been my imagination."

He went back into *Slave I*. Inside, all was silent, save for the sound of Anakin hammering and working away at the battered wing. Gingerly, Boba tended to his injured shoulder, cleaning the wound and putting on fresh bandages.

Then he set about repairing his body armor.

Ygabba and Gab'borah had given it to him back on Tatooine — Jango Fett's own Mandalorian body armor and combat boots. The armor had been damaged by General Grievous, but it could be fixed. Boba examined it carefully, then got out his own repair kit and touch-up paint.

It felt good to be fixing his armor. Somehow, it made it feel more like it was Boba's own.

It is *mine*, he thought, smoothing out a jagged spot where Grievous' energy blast had charred the plasteel. Then he began repainting the armor, a slightly darker color than that favored by Jango. As he did, he made a few other adjustments, tightening here, lengthening there.

Boba knew his father would be proud of him. And he also knew that his father would understand.

Boba was his own man now. He had accepted Jango Fett's legacy. Not just his helmet and armor, not just the book Jango had left him, but Jango's wisdom and skill, his discipline and determination. All of these things had made Boba who he was now —

One of the best bounty hunters in the galaxy.

But Boba wasn't content with that. As he shrugged into his armor and fastened it across his chest, he thought of Jabba the Hutt. Jabba paid well — for a Hutt, anyway — but Boba wanted to strike out on his own.

It's time, he thought, pulling on his helmet. He straightened and looked at the reflection in a mirror.

A pang shot through him at what he saw there. He felt loss and love and grief, but also pride.

I look like my father, he thought. *I wish . . . I wish he could see me. He would be proud of me. I know that.*

The mirror showed a tall, broad-shouldered figure, face masked by the battle helmet; but his bearing and strength plain for anyone to see —

Boba Fett.

And he wasn't merely Jabba's prize assassin. Soon, Boba Fett would be the best bounty hunter the galaxy had known —

Ever.

CHAPTER EIGHT

He strode back outside to check on Skywalker's repairs. In the doorway he paused again —

That sound, he thought. He listened, all his senses on edge. But the sound, whatever it was, had once again escaped him. He turned and hurried down to the moon's surface alongside his ship.

"How's it going?" Boba asked. He stooped to peer at *Slave I*'s wing.

"Just about done." Anakin wiped a spot of grease from his cheek and took a step back. "What do you think?"

Boba ran his hand across the wing, whistling softly. "Wow. You can hardly tell it was damaged at all."

"That's right," said Anakin with pride.

But somehow, Skywalker's pride no longer looked so much like arrogance. It looked more like satisfaction, even happiness. For a moment he stood and admired his own work. Then he turned to Boba.

Now it was Anakin's turn to be impressed.

"Your armor looks good," he said admiringly. "Your helmet, too."

Boba shrugged. "In my line of work, you need it."

"Yeah," said Anakin with a nod. " I can see that."

For a moment the two young men stood in silence.

At last Boba said, "Thanks for helping me with the repairs on my ship. But I have an important job to do —"

"So do I." Anakin cut him off. "You violated Republic airspace back there on Xagobah. All unauthorized personnel automatically become detainees of the Republic. You're in my charge now."

Boba's hand twitched toward his blaster. Anakin's did the same with his lightsaber. His steely eyes remained fixed on Boba.

"There's no point in resisting," Skywalker said calmly, though there was an edge of menace in his voice. "But I'll put in a good word for you —"

Boba's entire body tensed as he put himself into attack mode. Then he grimaced.

The injuries he'd sustained from Grievous were too great. Even as he moved, he could feel blood trickling from his wounded shoulder. The pain was excruciating — but he wouldn't let Skywalker know that.

"— after I bring you in for questioning," the Jedi finished. "I'm sure we can find a place for you to work within the Republic."

Boba's grimace deepened, though not from pain.

No way! he thought.

Working for the Republic was not an option. Working for anyone, except himself, was not an option! Jabba the Hutt might pay his bounties, but no one set limits on Boba Fett.

Not Jabba. Not the Republic.

And definitely not Anakin Skywalker.

But how to get away from the Jedi? Boba looked at the desolate moonscape surrounding them. Dunes, craters, depthless holes like horrible empty eyes or mouths on the lunar surface. He would find no refuge there.

No help, either . . .

He tried desperately to come up with a plan.

If only I hadn't taken such a hit from Grievous! he thought. He flinched, recalling the encounter that had nearly killed him — that would have killed him, if Boba hadn't managed to use his wits to escape. He glanced at Anakin.

I could take him, if I wasn't injured, he thought grimly. *And if he didn't have a Republic army at his beck and call! I could still take him. . . .*

As though the young Jedi could read Boba's mind, Anakin said, "Don't even think of escape, Fett. You're no match for me. Glynn-Beti's troop-ship is nearby. I'll bring you there, and she'll decide what's to be done with you."

"No —" Boba took a step toward Anakin. Skywalker's hand tightened around his weapon as Boba said, "I have a better idea."

Anakin regarded him suspiciously. "I warn you, if —"

"'If' nothing!" Boba snapped. "If you don't listen to me now, you're making a mistake."

Anakin's eyes narrowed. "What are you talking about?"

The bounty hunter hesitated. Since his father's death, Boba had been sustained by two things. One was a burning rage to take vengeance on his father's murderer, Mace Windu.

The other was a secret that only Boba knew. It was something he had learned back when he was on the toxic planet, Raxus Prime. He had been brought there by the bounty hunter Aurra Sing. She had been hired to capture Boba, by someone known as "the Count."

The Count was in fact the deadly Separatist leader Count Dooku, enemy of the Republic. He was a former Jedi Master, who, like Boba, now hated the Jedi. Unlike Boba, Dooku had allied himself with the Separatists.

Yet only Boba knew that Count Dooku was the same person as the mysterious Tyranus . . . the same Tyranus who had first approached Jango Fett to become the source for the Republic's clone army . . .

The same Tyranus who was therefore also helping the Republic!

Boba had kept this information secret from the Republic and the Jedi — until now. He had his Mandalorian armor, and his helmet. He had some of the most sophisticated weapons in the galaxy. And he had *Slave I*, the best ship in the galaxy.

But right now, he knew that none of these things was as valuable as what he knew about the Count. His knowledge of the Count's secret was also a weapon. And at the moment, it was a weapon more powerful than anything else Boba possessed. He drew himself up and stared coldly at Anakin Sky-walker.

Knowledge is power, his father had taught him. *Knowledge is a weapon — use it carefully, or pay the price!*

As he gazed at the threatening young Jedi before him, Boba hoped his knowledge wouldn't kill him.

CHAPTER NINE

Boba straightened and met Anakin's gaze.

"I have information vital to the safety of the Republic," Boba said.

Anakin stared at him in cold disbelief. "You what?"

"You heard me." Boba glared back at the Jedi. "What I know could mean the difference between the Republic's defeat — or ultimate victory."

Anakin's grasp on his weapon loosened, ever so slightly. "How do I know you're telling the truth?"

Boba shrugged. "You don't. But if I am, the Republic could have the knowledge it needs to defeat the Separatists. And if you don't make use of it, the Republic could be destroyed. Are you willing to take that chance?"

Boba watched Anakin carefully. Whatever this Jedi was, he wasn't a coward. Or stupid. Anakin shook his head.

"Why should I believe you? You're just a worth-less bounty hunter!"

"Not just any bounty hunter!" retorted Boba. "Think about it. You said that Obi-Wan Kenobi had spoken my name to you. Why would he bother telling you about me, unless I was important?"

Anakin frowned.

Got him there! thought Boba triumphantly. Before the Jedi could say more, Boba quickly went on.

"I need to go to Coruscant." The words were out almost before he knew what he was saying. But as soon as he did, he realized that they were right. "What I know can only be shared with the highest authority. If you try to stop me, you will be accused of treason."

"Coruscant?" For a second, Boba had the satisfaction of seeing Anakin's confidence falter. But only for an instant. "There's no place on Coruscant for a bounty hunter like you! No one will meet with you. No one important, anyway."

"That's where you're wrong," said Boba. Even as he spoke, he could feel his mouth go dry. He was taking a gamble, maybe the most perilous risk he had taken in his entire life. "Someone will meet me there. Someone important. Someone powerful . . ."

"Who?" demanded Anakin angrily.

Boba took a deep breath. He knew he was taking more than his luck in his hands.

He was taking his life.

Anakin took a step closer to Boba. "Tell me!"

Boba put his hand on his blaster, defying Anakin to come nearer.

"Supreme Chancellor Palpatine," he said.

Anakin froze. His eyes widened.

"The Chancellor?!"

Boba nodded. "That's right."

"But —"

Abruptly the world around them seemed to shatter. Rocks and waves of sand rained down. Boba shouted and dropped, scrambling for his blaster. Anakin fell, too. He rolled toward Boba, one arm raised protectively above the two of them.

"It's a space slug!" Anakin yelled. "Stay down!"

From a crater behind the Jedi starfighter, a vast shape emerged, blotting out the sky above them. Its huge, snakelike body shot through the air, boulders and great rocks flying everywhere in its wake. Its huge mouth yawned open, showing rows of teethlike blades as it twisted and lunged —

Straight toward Boba and Anakin!

Boba ducked, just in time, as a displaced boulder hurtled past him. The space slug roared.

"This'll slow it!" shouted Anakin. He stood and grabbed for his lightsaber. But before he could draw it, a man-sized rock came hurtling toward him.

The rock smashed against Anakin. With a strangled cry, the young Jedi fell.

"Skywalker!" Boba shouted.

But he had no time to help the wounded Jedi.

The space slug was upon them!

Boba hefted his powerful DC-15 blaster. It lacked the scope of his bigger weapons, but he was in close range to his target now —

Very close!

"*WHHHOOOORAAAAAGGGH!*" the space slug roared. It was close enough that Boba could feel its hot breath, stinking of scorched rock and sand. And it was heading right toward *Slave I*!

"Get away from my ship!" Boba yelled furiously. He darted to one side of *Slave I*, stooping to pick up a rock. He hurled it at the predator.

THUNK!

The rock struck the predatory monster on its most vulnerable part — its eye.

"*RRRUAAAGHRRRR!*"

With a thunderous growl of pain and rage, the

space slug changed its course in midair. It veered away from Boba's ship — and the fallen Anakin — and surged in full pursuit of the bounty hunter!

Boba ran toward a small crater. It was way too small to hide Boba for more than a moment or two.

But that was all the time Boba needed to take aim. He crouched, his blaster leveled. He got a fix on the space slug's head — which was rapidly approaching!

"Can't miss!" Boba muttered through gritted teeth. From the corner of his eye he could see Anakin turn, groaning, and stumble to his feet. "Otherwise we're both dead — and I've got a score to settle with another Jedi!"

Once again the space slug's deafening roar rang out. Fragments of rock fell around Boba as the serpentine creature reared above him.

BAAMMMM!

Boba fired a direct hit — right between the eyes!

"GLOOORB!" The gigantic slug's roar rose to a bubbling shriek of pain. Its head swayed back and forth, giving Boba another chance to fire — and another!

"Yes!" Boba crowed.

Two more hits! The space slug writhed in agony.

Its knife-edged teeth clashed as it recoiled from the bounty hunter. Greenish blood spattered Boba as the space slug retreated with a long, bubbling cry, sliding back into its hole.

"Yuck!" exclaimed Boba, wiping slug goo from his body armor. "Just after I got it all cleaned up, too!" He sheathed his weapon then removed his helmet, checking it for damage. Then he hurried toward his ship.

"That was pretty good."

Boba froze in his tracks. A few feet away Anakin stood, staring at him intently. Boba knew the Jedi was deciding what to do about him.

But he couldn't know what was going on in Skywalker's head. Did it matter that he'd just saved the Jedi's life? That this was the second time he'd saved a Jedi since he'd started the hunt for Wat Tambor?

Anakin shook his head, then looked Boba up and down as he approached.

"Yeah, that was pretty good," the Jedi repeated. "Not bad at all, considering."

"Considering what?" snapped Boba. He stared challengingly at Skywalker. Boba really didn't want to draw arms against this particular Jedi — but he wouldn't hesitate if he had to.

"Considering you're getting ready to set your course for Coruscant," said Anakin.

"Huh?" It took a moment for the words to sink in. When they did, Boba allowed himself a small smile.

Yes!

But Boba was careful not to let his true emotions show outside of his mask. He had another, secret motive for going to Coruscant. And Skywalker could never learn what that was.

"Yes. You can go to Coruscant — under these conditions," added Anakin. He gave *Slave I*'s repaired wing one last careful look. Then he headed toward his starfighter.

"I'll give you the coordinates," Anakin continued. "And the signal for takeoff. I'm handing you over to Governor Tarkin. He'll escort you to the Chancellor. If you don't like those conditions, you're history. When you enter Coruscant airspace, follow his lead. And your weapons have to remain on your ship."

Boba bristled. "Why?" he asked angrily. "I'm not your prisoner!"

"No, you're not. But he knows Coruscant, and you don't. I know who can be trusted —"

"I trust nobody," said Boba. Already he had a plan for what he would really do on Coruscant.

His eyes met Anakin's unflinchingly. "No one but myself."

Anakin looked at him. Then he nodded, turning to ready his ship for departure.

"We have a lot in common, Boba Fett," he said as he clambered into his starfighter. "Perhaps we'll meet again."

CHAPTER TEN

Coruscant!

Far below *Slave I*, the glittering planet stretched like a vast computer circuit, blinking and glowing with thousands of domes, towers, skyscrapers, airspeeders. The high-rises lifted into the sky, their brilliant lights blazing gold and silver and scarlet. The hazy atmosphere seemed bathed in eternal sunset. It was beautiful and impressive and very, very big.

Boba had never been to Coruscant. He knew that the planet was covered by a single vast metropolis, Galactic City. Galactic City housed the galactic government, overseen by Chancellor Palpatine. And in the shadow of Galactic City's looming towers sprawled the planet's great underworld. This was a seedy place where criminals held sway. Boba knew of it from Jabba the Hutt. The Hutt clan controlled a good part of Coruscant's black market, though a petty crime lord named Hat Lo managed things for them.

But something else was on Coruscant, too, something even more important to Boba —

The Jedi Temple, where the Jedi High Council met — and where Mace Windu could be found.

"Mace is a senior member of the High Council," Boba said to himself. "He will have dealings with Palpatine. Somehow I'll use Palpatine to get to Mace Windu. And then . . ."

Boba thought of his father, slain by Windu. "And then, Father, we will be avenged," he said softly. He promised himself this would be the one exception to the bounty hunter law he had established for himself. Never would he kill on his own time — except this time. For honor's sake.

He sat at *Slave I*'s console. Not far away, Governor Tarkin's starship hovered, awaiting landing clearance. But Boba had already made contact with someone who had deeper ties to Coruscant than Anakin Skywalker.

"Boba Fett!" A voice crackled through the interior of *Slave I*. Seconds later a face filled the ship's viewscreen. It was the oily figure of Hat Lo, his pudgy frame encased in heavy protective shielding. "What brings you here?"

"Business," said Boba tersely. Hat Lo liked to think that he was in charge of the Coruscant underworld. Boba knew better. Jabba was really in charge of things here. Hat Lo was merely his lackey.

Hat Lo wasn't too smart, either. He'd be easy to exploit — if Boba was careful. "I have a few things to tend to," said the bounty hunter.

"Hunting, eh?" A flicker of unease crossed Hat Lo's overfed face. "Er, what kind of things are you tending to?"

"That's my business. And Jabba's," Boba added pointedly.

"Jabba! Of course, of course," blathered the man on the viewscreen. "I had no idea —"

Boba watched in satisfaction as Hat Lo's fat face grew a shade paler. "I know I can count on you for any assistance I need while I'm here," said Boba.

"Absolutely!" Hat Lo nearly groveled as he spoke. "Anything Jabba needs — er, anything *you* need —"

"Good. I'll be in touch soon," said Boba shortly, and ended the transmission.

Almost immediately Governor Tarkin's voice echoed through *Slave I.*

"We're cleared," he announced in a tone that

Boba already felt sounded sinister. "We've received permission to land at the Jedi Temple, thanks to General Skywalker — that way you won't have to go through Coruscant security. Just let me do all the talking — and remember: no weapons."

"Right," growled Boba. He was glad he was wearing his helmet, so that Tarkin wouldn't see his anger at the request once they landed. "No weapons . . ."

None when he set foot on Coruscant, anyway. But once Boba was ready to leave Coruscant —

That would be another story.

They touched down on the broad, open landing platform of the Jedi Temple. Tarkin's vessel landed first, *Slave I* less than a minute later. From inside, Boba watched as a single slender figure clad in the Jedi's distinctive robes crossed to greet the governor, who was a rising star, it seemed, in the Clone Wars. Boba waited until the two were engaged in conversation. Then he quickly readied himself to join them.

But first he had to remove his weapons.

"I hate to leave you behind," he said with regret.

"But I better not take any chances. I'm so close to finding Mace Windu — don't want to blow it now."

He removed the Westar-34 blasters from his weapons belt and his knee holsters, and put them safely away. Then he did the same with his missiles and dart shooter.

But he didn't remove the blades in his gauntlets. And he didn't remove his jet pack.

"Not even the Jedi can force me to visit a strange planet with no self-defense whatsoever," Boba muttered. "And when I see Hat Lo, I can get some new weapons. It's time I upgraded a few items, anyway."

He made sure his helmet was in place. Then he did a last minute check of *Slave I*.

"Okay," Boba said to himself. He stood in his ship's doorway and looked out. His heart began to pound, not with fear but anticipation. *I'm on the Jedi's home turf now! Got to be careful. Got to be calm. Got to be ready —*

To find and defeat Mace Windu!

CHAPTER ELEVEN

As Boba strode across the open plaza, the strange Jedi turned to appraise the newcomer. Her eyes beneath her somber brown hood were alert and questioning.

"Who is this you have brought here?" she asked Tarkin. "I know that I approved your request to land, but you gave us so few details. . . ."

The governor waited for Boba to join them, then turned to the older Jedi and bowed his head to her respectfully. He looked at Boba and gestured at the tall Jedi.

"This is Luminara Unduli," Tarkin said by way of introduction. "I have worked with her before, in various negotiations with the Separatists."

Luminara Unduli regarded Boba with interest. She had the dark eyes and smooth bronze skin and ornate facial tattoos of the desert-dwellers of Miral. She had their detached intelligence as well.

Even inside his helmet, Boba could feel the intensity of her probing gaze.

"So, Governor Tarkin. This is the envoy Skywalker mentioned." Her stare grew even more pronounced.

Boba's hand began to twitch instinctively for his blaster, but he checked it in time. Instead he inclined his head to Luminara and said nothing.

"Does the envoy have a name?" Luminara asked pointedly. "I note he does not have a face. Not one I can see, anyway."

"The envoy has news for the Chancellor alone," Tarkin said smoothly. He glanced aside, and Boba could swear he winked at him. "He wishes to remain anonymous. His mission is extremely perilous. His journey has been arduous. And he may have information that will help our cause. The Republic has guaranteed him safe passage here — that should be enough to satisfy the Jedi High Council."

"And do you take responsibility for him?" Luminara asked coolly. "These are perilous times for all of us."

"No doubt," concluded Tarkin. Boba could see the governor's eyes flash dangerously. "I have spoken for him. My word shall be enough."

Luminara's gaze flickered at Tarkin's words; with anger or doubt, Boba could not be sure. Finally, she nodded. "Very well. I can see he is unarmed. I will trust the Chancellor's judgment, Governor. You may show him to his chambers."

She began to turn to leave. Then she stopped, adding, "The Chancellor has acknowledged your request that he meet with this envoy. He has agreed to do so tonight. Chancellor Palpatine must meet with Mace Windu in his chambers first. You may escort your *envoy* to his rooms now. Then I need to debrief you on the Xagobah situation, Governor."

Tarkin bowed. Boba inclined his head very slightly as Luminara left. He was really glad now that they couldn't see his face.

Mace Windu!

Boba would never get another chance like this. Not even the thought of Chancellor Palpatine's wrath could curb Boba's fierce joy at the thought of destroying his enemy.

Gotta find Hat Lo first, though, he thought. *Gotta get new weapons — and shake Tarkin!*

The governor seemed preoccupied with his own thoughts. "This way," he said. He motioned Boba to follow him. "I'll take you to your quarters. Then I must take care of some Senate affairs."

They walked in silence across the landing plaza. Ahead of them loomed the proud spires of the Jedi Temple. As they drew nearer, Boba had to fight the urge to draw a nonexistent blaster. He could see dark-robed figures moving around the base of the closest tower. A few of them glanced curiously at him.

"They better not give me any trouble," Boba muttered under his breath.

"They won't," Tarkin said curtly.

They had reached one of the main entrances to the Temple. Tarkin slowed his steps. He looked at the young bounty hunter beside him.

"I'm taking an awful risk with you, Boba Fett," he said in a low voice. "And I'm not even sure why. But I have an enormous amount of confidence in young Skywalker."

Tarkin gestured for Boba to enter the Temple.

"I hope you prove worth it," Tarkin said. "We are always looking for new allies."

Boba watched as Governor Tarkin walked off into his own future. Then Boba turned, and silently entered the stronghold of the Jedi.

CHAPTER TWELVE

Inside the Jedi Temple, all was muted, but not utterly silent. Robed Jedi passed, their cloaks sweeping the floor. A small group of very young Jedi initiates went by, walking in a straight line. They turned to stare with open mouths at the tall, helmeted young man who strode past them.

"Who is that?" one of the children asked. The Jedi instructor leading them paused, staring at Boba curiously.

"I'm looking for the visitors' quarters," Boba said before she could question him. "Anakin Skywalker arranged for me to stay here."

At mention of Skywalker's name, the Jedi nodded.

"Of course," she said. "That way — follow the corridor until it turns left. The door of your room will be open."

"Thanks," said Boba. The children continued to

stare at him with such huge eyes that he was tempted to laugh.

But he didn't. Instead he hurried down the corridor the Jedi had indicated. It was a wide passage, lit with the bright, soft light the Jedi favored for public spaces. In the distance he could see two formidable figures walking side by side, deep in discussion. As they drew near, Boba stiffened.

It can't be! he thought. Every hair on his head prickled. Without thinking his hand grasped at his utility belt.

That was when Boba remembered that his weapons were gone.

And only a handsbreadth away was —

Mace Windu!

Boba's mouth went dry. The last time he had seen Windu was in the Geonosian execution arena. There the Jedi Master had stood unflinching and grim above the corpse of Boba's father, Jango, whom he had slain.

Father! Boba thought, as the anguish of that moment came back to him.

As though he had spoken the words aloud, Boba saw Windu suddenly glance his way.

Can't let him know it's me! Boba thought desperately. *Not now. Not when I'm so close!*

Boba hadn't seen Mace Windu in many years. But he knew of the tall Jedi Master's incredible skill at fighting — and more. Windu was rumored to possess a voice and will so powerful that he seldom needed to use the Force on his enemies, let alone a lightsaber.

And that voice had fallen suddenly, ominously, silent as Boba passed in the hallway.

Don't stare at him, Boba thought. *Just keep going. Don't stop, don't —*

But he could feel Mace Windu's gaze boring into him. And he could see Windu halt, putting a hand on his companion's arm as he gazed after Boba.

"Who —?" Mace Windu began to ask in his deep tones.

"Master Windu! Master Windu!"

A child's high voice rang through the passage. The Jedi Master turned, his expression changing from suspicion to amusement as one of the tiny Jedi younglings ran toward him, the breathless instructor at her heels.

"Veda!" the instructor called in exasperation. "Get back here immediately!"

"But I want to ask him something!"

Mace looked at the child. As he laughed, Boba hastened on down the passage. Still, as the hall began to turn toward the left, he couldn't resist glancing back.

Mace stood, listening patiently as the child prattled on. But as he listened he slowly turned his head, staring directly down the passage.

At Boba.

He can't know it's me, Boba thought. *And even if he does —*

For an instant Boba remained where he was. The Jedi could not see the hatred in his eyes.

But perhaps he could feel the hatred in Boba's soul.

"I'll see you again very soon, Mace Windu," Boba whispered before turning to continue on his way.

The room that had been made ready for him was spare but comfortable. He had worried that the Jedi were going to put a guard on watch, but clearly they were too occupied to spend effort on an informant whose information they did not know yet to be true. But this played to Boba's advantage. He wasted little time in his room. He shut the door and activated the room's communicator. Within seconds, Hat Lo's sweaty face once more stared out at him.

"Boba!" he said in forced joviality. "I didn't expect to hear again from you so soon!"

"No? Well, you're going to see me even sooner. I need to meet with you."

"Now?" Hat Lo sounded aggrieved.

"As I told you, my business is urgent. Jabba's business . . ."

Boba let his voice trail off threateningly.

Hat Lo blanched. "Of course, of course!" he said. "I'll send a speeder for you immediately! I will meet you within the hour at the Sign of the Tri-Forked Tongue. You will be my most honored guest," he added, his voice rising with anxiety. "As befits one of Jabba's most trusted circle — besides myself, of course."

"Of course," said Boba. Behind his helmet he smiled unpleasantly. "The Sign of the Tri-Forked Tongue, in one hour. I'll see you there."

Hat Lo's round face blipped from view. For a few minutes Boba sat alone in his room.

"Mace's lightsaber assaults are legendary," he said, brooding. "He's taller than me, too, though not by much. I have my blades, but I'll need a blaster. And a saberdart would be really good for backup. . . ."

Boba nodded excitedly at the thought of the poisonous Kamino weapon. *That would really do the job! Not even a Jedi Master could withstand the venom of a saberdart! Now let's just hope Hat Lo can put his grimy little hands on one for me.*

He hurried off to meet the Coruscant lowlife's airspeeder.

CHAPTER THIRTEEN

The bright-red airspeeder was waiting near *Slave I* on the landing dock. With a pang, Boba immediately recognized the humanoid alien piloting it.

"Oh no!" he groaned. "Not Elan Sleazebaggano!"

"Elan's the name," the obnoxious young con man announced as Boba jumped into the seat beside him. His long antennae wriggled with pride. "Flying's my game! Unless, of course, I could interest you in some Polordion smootdust?"

Elan whipped out a shimmering green parcel and waved it enticingly in Boba's face. "One hundred percent pure, satisfaction guaranteed —"

Boba grabbed Elan's shoulder. "I'm not interested in your cheap contraband, Sleazebaggano!" he said. "Take me to the Sign of the Tri-Forked Tongue — fast!"

Elan nodded eagerly. "Sure, sure!" The shimmering green packet disappeared. Elan punched at the control panels. The airspeeder swooped away from the docking platform.

"You look like a discerning bounty hunter," Elan went on, almost without drawing a breath. "Maybe you're more interested in a pair of tortapo-shell shades! One-hundred-percent natural, guaranteed to block out dangerous infradig rays —"

"Fast, and silent!" ordered Boba. He tightened his grip on Elan's shoulder.

"Sure, sure!" gulped Elan. His long fleshy antennae twitched nervously. "I live to please. But maybe you'd consider —"

Boba groaned. Elan was relentless!

Where's my blaster when I need it?

"This better be a short trip," Boba said menacingly. "Otherwise . . ."

"Sure, sure!"

The airspeeder raced away from the Jedi Temple. Around them the skyrise caverns of Coruscant shone and glittered. This was where the galaxy's most wealthy residents lived. Senators, ambassadors, diplomats, guild leaders, merchants — all in those glimmering towers. That was who rode in those sleek speeder limos. That was who ate in those fantastically expensive restaurant terraces, and slept in bedrooms bigger than a Caridan training arena.

Boba tried not to look impressed by it all.

But as they approached the gigantic building that housed the Galactic Senate, he couldn't help it. His eyes widened slightly, and he edged closer to the side of the airspeeder to get a better look.

"So that's it," he murmured. The domed building was immense — it looked as though it could be half the size of the moon where he'd met Anakin. "That's where Chancellor Palpatine holds court. And tomorrow . . ."

He couldn't voice the rest of his thought out loud. Tomorrow, Mace Windu would be dead. Boba would be long gone from here. Supreme Chancellor Palpatine would be addressing the Senate in an urgent emergency meeting to share with them the secret that Boba had shared with him — that Dooku and Tyranus were the same person.

One who wanted the Republic to fall.

"The Senate Building, that's right," said Elan. He barely gave the huge domed edifice a second look. "That's where all the galaxy's most important official business takes place. But where we're going —"

The airspeeder gave a sudden lurch. Without warning it dived straight down between kilometer-high buildings, as though it was plunging into a shining abyss.

"Watch it!" shouted Boba as another speeder streaked right toward them. He grabbed the controls from Elan. "We're going to crash right into —"

At the last possible moment, Boba got their speeder to veer sharply to one side. He had a glimpse of the angry, white-faced pilot of the other speeder glaring at Elan's bright-red one.

Then Elan calmly removed Boba's hands from the controls.

"Where we're going," Elan went on as though nothing had happened, "is where the galaxy's most important unofficial business takes place. Coruscant underground!"

"You're talking about the gangland underworld," Boba said. He watched as they sped down, down toward the garishly lit lower levels of Galactic City. "Hat Lo's territory."

"And mine!" Elan said in a wounded tone. "I happen to be the provider of the very finest death sticks in the galaxy, very reasonably priced, very —"

"Stop!" shouted Boba. "Get me to the Tri-Forked Tongue. NOW!"

The rest of their trip passed in near silence. Now and then Elan sighed noisily. And his antennae never stopped wriggling, as though they were trying to sell Boba on some highly illegal Nkllonian Lava Extract, one hundred percent pure.

But at last the red airspeeder began to slow. Ahead of them beckoned a brilliant entryway, lit by gaudy purple and green zeon light-tubes. The VR image of a slithering Monga serpent repeatedly rose and seemed to strike, its mouth opening to display three long furling orange tongues.

"The Sign of the Tri-Forked Tongue," Elan announced. He sounded bored. "I don't know why you're bothering with this place. No one goes here anymore."

"Well, I do," snapped Boba.

He extricated himself from the airspeeder. In the shadows, a slavering corridor ghoul crouched, looking for unwary visitors to prey on. A group of sinister-looking, emaciated mutants stood near the club's entrance, playing pillel-dice. It seemed like an unpromising place to obtain illegal weapons.

But Boba had no time to look for a better one. He wanted Mace Windu dead — tonight.

"My card," said Elan. He handed Boba a shining strip of crimson emblazoned with the words _ELAN_

"In the event that Hat Lo is unable to provide you with what you need, please don't hesitate to call me."

"Unlikely," retorted Boba.

But he took the card.

The airspeeder roared off, careering wildly between alarmed passersby. Boba turned and looked at the seedy club before him.

Hat Lo better be there! he thought grimly. *I can't afford to waste any more time.*

He entered the Sign of the Tri-Forked Tongue. Inside was even dimmer and grimier than the colorful VR sign had promised. Underfoot, something sticky and unpleasant clung to Boba's boots.

"Ugh!" he said, kicking at a small pulsating object — a young granite slug. The slug exploded with a blubbering sound. Bits of goo flecked the walls.

Boba grimaced. "Great. This isn't a very good start."

A few meters farther on, a burly figure blocked a doorway, a six-limbed alien with protruding eyes. Beside it stood a slender Twi'lek, yawning.

"I'm here to see Hat Lo," Boba announced gruffly. The tan-and-brown-striped Twi'lek blinked, then quietly slipped away. The alien bouncer glanced at a list in one of its hands and waved Boba in.

The Sign of the Tri-Forked Tongue was dim and smoky. It was filled with small tables where Coruscant's riffraff sat, gambling and arranging illegal deals, angrily settling old scores and making new ones.

"There he is," Boba muttered.

He spotted Hat Lo at a table in the corner. The would-be crime boss was surrounded by five Codru-Ji bodyguards. Two of them were adults, in their four-armed, humanoid mode. The remaining three were juveniles, in the Codru-Ji's distinctive four-legged wyrwulf stage.

None of them appeared to be very happy to see Boba approaching their boss's table.

"Hat Lo," Boba said. He glanced disdainfully at the bodyguards. "I need to talk to you — alone."

The crook's round face shone with sweat. He maneuvered awkwardly in his body shielding.

"Make room for Boba Fett," he ordered, gesturing impatiently for the bodyguards to move. "Boba, please — sit."

Boba stood his ground. "Not until they leave."

His hand moved threateningly toward where his

blaster should be. He was unarmed, but in the darkness, it would be difficult for anyone to know that.

Hat Lo regarded the bounty hunter uneasily. Finally he commanded his bodyguards, "Go! Wait for me by the door!"

The pack of Codru-Ji stood. They strode across the room, the young wyrwulfs casting hungry looks back at Boba.

"Sit, sit," repeated Hat Lo. As if by magic, the slender Twi'lek appeared at his shoulder. She carried two beakers of fizzing liquid. Hat Lo took one. The Twi'lek offered the other to Boba.

"Drink with me!" exclaimed Hat Lo. He raised his beaker and waited for Boba to do the same. "To friendship!"

"No thanks," said Boba. He dumped the beaker's contents onto the floor. An acrid smell rose from the ground, followed by a puff of greenish flame and a sizzling noise. "Dozoisian Snark Venom. Deadly if it passes your lips. Nice try, Hat Lo."

Hat Lo feigned surprise.

"I'm shocked, shocked," he said. "It's poisonous?"

He shoved his still-full beaker back at the Twi'lek, glaring at her as she beat a hasty retreat.

Then he turned back to Boba, shrugging as if to say, *You can't blame a crook for trying!*

"Well then," the two-bit gangster continued. "Now that we've gotten the preliminaries out of the way, what can I do for you?"

"I need to upgrade my armaments," said Boba. He sat opposite Hat Lo, keeping a careful eye out for the bodyguards.

"Of course. And for some reason you can't go through legal channels." Hat Lo leered. "Well, you've come to the right person! May I ask what brings you to Coruscant?"

Boba hesitated. He was reluctant to share the truth with Hat Lo. But his minions could probably find out any information Hat Lo needed to know.

And Boba didn't want any unnecessary attention being drawn to him in the next few hours. . . .

If he told Hat Lo himself, Boba could control the situation. And Boba liked being in control.

"I have business with Supreme Chancellor Palpatine," he said.

Boba was rewarded by Hat Lo's look of stunned dismay. "Palpatine? But that's — well, that's extremely interesting." Hat Lo's beady little eyes narrowed. "And you're looking for weapons? Why? Not even Jabba the Hutt can be thinking of assassinating the Supreme Chancellor!"

Boba shook his head. "Jabba's plans are no business of yours, Hat Lo. Not unless you want to be implicated in them . . ."

He let the words hang in the air as a threat. Hat Lo raised his hands defensively. "No, no! Such important matters are far too big for a mere hardworking businessman like myself! I ask only because one hears rumors. Unpleasant rumors. Great changes are afoot, Boba Fett. You should be careful what side you're on, when the changes come."

"I'm on no one's side," said Boba sharply. "I trust no one but myself. And I certainly don't trust you, Hat Lo! So don't try to cheat me, or sell me substandard weapons."

"The thought never crossed my mind," replied Hat Lo. Still, he looked disappointed. "Now, what exactly do you need?"

Boba rolled off his requests. "A Westar blaster, some missiles, and pulse grenades, to start with."

Hat Lo shook his head. "I have none of those at the moment. If I'd known in advance, perhaps. But at such short notice? No. You understand, my business is supply-driven. Here on Coruscant, we try to settle things more, shall I say, quietly."

"More underhandedly, you mean?" sneered Boba.

"I mean we try not to draw unwanted attention to ourselves by frivolous use of weapons. Not that your weapons could ever be deemed frivolous," Hat Lo added quickly. "Now, what I do have at the moment is a flechette pistol — very nice, never been used, fully loaded. Also some cryo-ban grenades, if you'd like."

Boba looked impressed. "A flechette? Those are hard to come by!"

"I know," Hat Lo said with pride. "Are you familiar with their use?"

Boba snorted. A good bounty hunter made use of whatever weapons came his way — and Boba wasn't just a good bounty hunter. He was the best!

"Of course I know how to use it!" The pistol released canisters holding hundreds of tiny, razor-edged blades — flechettes. "I'll take them all, and whatever else you have."

A short while later the deal was done. The Twi'lek materialized again, this time accompanied by a shifty-looking Bothan carrying the weapons. Boba examined them all carefully, then nodded.

"These will do."

Hat Lo dismissed his lackeys. Boba began arming

himself, being careful to keep the weapons concealed on his body armor. After a few minutes, Hat Lo discreetly cleared his throat.

"Ahem. A small matter, of course — but how do you intend to pay for these?"

Behind his helmet, Boba's eyes glittered dangerously. He looked around at the interior of the seedy club.

"I don't recall seeing the Sign of the Tri-Forked Tongue listed among Jabba's holdings here on Coruscant," he said. "I wonder what Jabba would say if he knew you owned it, and were skimming off the profits, rather than giving them to him?"

Hat Lo began to splutter. "That's — that's not true! This is a mere sideline for me! Something for my old age —"

Boba made as though to leave.

"Wait!" cried Hat Lo. Boba stared at him, then slowly sat back down. "Of course, I had no intention of charging you for these weapons! Consider them a gift, to you — and to Jabba."

Boba nodded. "Very well."

"And please, tell Jabba where you got them! And assure him of my devotion, and my undying loyalty!"

"Undying sleaziness is more like it," said Boba.

He got to his feet. This time he really was ready to go. He saw Hat Lo's many-armed bodyguards watching him from across the room. But not even a bunch of angry Codru-Ji would dare mess with Boba Fett, now that he was fully armed.

Which reminded him of something. He turned back to Hat Lo.

"One last thing," Boba said. "Do you know where I could get my hands on a saberdart?"

"A saberdart?" Hat Lo's eyes narrowed. He pursed his lips, then shook his head. "They're outlawed here on Coruscant these days. Everyone's too worried about attacks on the Senators."

"Right." Boba nodded and turned away. "I'll give Jabba a decent report, Hat Lo — unless you give me reason to do otherwise."

The petty crime boss watched him go. "A pleasure doing business with you, Boba Fett," he croaked, then laughed hoarsely. "I'm sure our paths will cross again!"

"Maybe," said Boba under his breath.

He swaggered past the Codru-Ji, back out onto the streets of Coruscant's underworld.

CHAPTER FOURTEEN

Boba hadn't thought about how he was going to get back up to the Jedi Temple to track down Mace Windu.

But as soon as he walked out of the Sign of the Tri-Forked Tongue, a familiar sight greeted him.

A shining red airspeeder hovered near the club's entrance.

"Yo! Wassup!" Elan Sleazebaggano gestured for Boba to hop in beside him. "Come on, I'll take you back!"

Dismayed, Boba looked around. He saw the corridor ghoul nosing at what looked unpleasantly like a body. He saw two Mantellian savrips fighting over what looked like another body. He saw a group of space pirates exchanging greetings near a darkened doorway.

What he didn't see was another vehicle of any kind.

"Come on!" urged Elan. "I'll get you there faster than anyone can!"

"All right," Boba said, resigned. He climbed into the airspeeder, glowering at Elan. "But if you try to sell me something, Sleazebaggano, you're dead!"

"Sell you something?" Elan yanked at the controls. With a squeal, the airspeeder shot up through the high-rise canyons of Coruscant. "I wouldn't dream of selling you something! Especially not something highly illegal and fatally toxic, like a saberdart."

"A saberdart?" Boba held tight to his seat, as the airspeeder narrowly avoided slamming into a building. "You have a saberdart?"

"I never said that," Elan replied. The airspeeder shot past another speeder full of willowy young Dathomir witches. Elan waved at them. "Girls! Hellooooo!"

The witches stared back in ill-disguised disgust. The red airspeeder rocketed upward, as Elan continued.

"I never said that, because to possess a saberdart is a criminal offense. And I, of course, am a respected member of Coruscant's business community. But yes, I do have one."

Elan took one hand from the controls. The airspeeder wobbled dangerously as he seemed to pluck something from thin air. The object glittered, as Elan turned and handed it to Boba.

"One saberdart, no waiting. No payment, either — consider it a gift, a token of my great admiration for your bounty-hunting skills. Oh, you might mention it to Jabba, if you feel inclined," said Elan. "Put in a good word for me. A word to the wise, as they say."

Boba took the saberdart. He looked at it suspiciously, but it seemed to be genuine.

"How did you —" he began, but Elan cut him off.

"I'd tell you," he said, "but then you'd have to kill me. Trust me, it's real."

In the near distance, the Jedi Temple's towers loomed. The airspeeder began to slow. Quickly Boba shoved the dart onto his utility belt.

The speeder came to a stop on the docking platform. Boba climbed out.

"Thanks," he said grudgingly.

"Anytime!" said Elan. He looked up at Boba and wiggled his antennae. "Just remember — tell your friends! Tell your enemies! I stand behind all my products! One-hundred-percent pure, satisfaction guaranteed!"

With a farewell wave of his antennae, Elan

powered up his vehicle. The bright-red airspeeder shot into reverse. Then it rocketed off into the haze.

Boba watched it go. Then he turned and hurried toward the Temple entrance.

Got to find Mace Windu, he thought with iron determination. His hands traced over his flechette pistol and his concealed daggers. Last of all he checked that the saberdart was where it could be easily deployed. *Got to finish something that Mace Windu started, a long time ago.*

And then — then it will be time to start on a new life.

Because once he had avenged his father's death, Boba knew he would be ready to take Jango's place in the world. Not as a boy, but as a man.

He saw *Slave I* waiting in its docking bay.

"I'll be back soon," he said, smiling slightly at sight of his ship. As he passed, he reached to touch the wing that Anakin Skywalker had fixed. "When I return, the sky's the limit."

Then, silent and unseen, Boba Fett entered the Jedi Temple.

The final hunt for Mace Windu had begun.

CHAPTER FIFTEEN

It was early evening now. Most of the Jedi were at meals, or tending to private weapons practice, or research in the Archives library. Boba made his way quickly and stealthily through the Temple's winding passages.

Word must have passed among the Jedi that Boba was here on official business and was not to be detained. The few Jedi he passed scarcely gave him a look.

"Typical Jedi arrogance," Boba murmured.

He felt almost disappointed that no one confronted him. He'd like to take out a few Jedi on their own turf!

Still, Boba knew he had no time to waste on anyone but Mace Windu.

I'll have plenty of other chances to take out Jedi scum, he thought. *First things first!*

It didn't take him long to figure out where the

members of the Jedi Council had their quarters. It took him even less time to find an alcove housing a worn door. He opened the door carefully and peeked inside.

"A service corridor!" said Boba under his breath. "Just what I needed!"

He checked to make sure no one saw him, and slipped inside. The passage was completely empty and smelled of dust. A few dead Coruscant botflies were scattered on the floor, but nothing else. Boba checked the walls, then took a few scans using one of his handheld nav aids.

"Yes!" gloated Boba.

The tiny computer showed a grid of red and green lines: a map of the Council Members level. The secondary passage he stood inside was a disused corridor that ran parallel to the central hallway.

If I follow this passage, it will lead me straight to Mace Windu's chambers. I just have to get there before he leaves for his meeting with Palpatine!

Boba shoved the nav aid back into his utility belt. Then he stealthily began to run, his feet making no sound in the narrow passage. In a few minutes he had reached the next level, then the next.

Finally he saw another door in the shadows. His footsteps slowed.

"Got to be careful here," he whispered.

This door led to the corridor that went directly to Mace Windu's chambers.

But Boba certainly didn't want to meet Windu where others might see them and come to the Jedi's aid. Very slowly he cracked the door open and peered out.

The corridor was empty. Ruby-colored light slanted down from viewscreens high overhead. Outside, it was sunset on Coruscant.

Boba looked around carefully. Then he quickly slipped into the central passage. He ran without a sound to where the hallway ended. There, a single black doorway loomed.

The door to Mace Windu's chambers. The door to Mace Windu's death!

Boba slid his hand over the flechette pistol. He looked over his shoulder to see if anyone had spotted him.

No one was there.

Slowly Boba drew the pistol. He cocked its safety, then crept toward the door. Moments from now, he would confront his enemy.

Mace would be deep in thought, preparing himself for his meeting with the Supreme Chancellor. He would be stunned to see Boba burst into his room. He would have no chance to defend himself. Not even a lightsaber could deflect hundreds of flechettes!

And not even a Jedi could withstand the deadly toxins released by a saberdart.

Boba's hand was on the door. His heart pounded as he took a deep breath.

He thought of his father, Jango, lying decapitated in the arena. He thought of Mace Windu lying dead. He recalled Jango's face breaking into a rare smile as he read to his son in their home on Geonosis.

"This is for you, Father," whispered Boba. He raised the flechette pistol.

Then, with all his strength he pushed the door open. Weapon ready to fire, Boba Fett lunged inside the Jedi's chamber, and found himself face-to-face with —

Nothing.

CHAPTER SIXTEEN

It can't be!

Boba looked around in frustrated rage. The chamber was empty. He swiveled, his pistol ready to fire, and looked around.

There was no one. Even without checking the rest of the room, Boba's hyperalert senses registered the truth.

The Jedi Master was gone.

Boba quickly sheathed his weapon. He strode to a round, low cushion of the type favored by high-ranking Jedi, stooped, and laid a hand upon it.

It was still warm. Windu must have left just minutes before.

Boba fought a surge of fury. He'd been so close!

But he wasn't going to let Mace get away so easily. Boba knew where he was bound — to his private meeting with Palpatine in the Senate Building. Boba had no idea where in that vast building he might track down Windu.

But Boba had no doubt that he would succeed in finding him. He turned and started for the door, then stopped.

Too dangerous to go back out there now. Someone might see me and alert Windu. . . .

He drew the door closed. He began a quick search of the chamber, looking for something that might be useful.

A minute later he found it — a small monitor tucked into the wall. Boba activated it, then brought up the most recently viewed screen.

"Got it!" he crowed.

The screen showed an itinerary, generated by the Supreme Chancellor's office. There was a reminder of the time for Mace Windu's private meeting, just fifteen minutes from now. There was a memo regarding the meeting's topic.

EXTREMELY URGENT was all that Boba bothered to read before scrolling down.

And there was a map of the Senate Building, showing the exact location of Palpatine's antechamber, where the meeting would be held!

"Perfect," said Boba. He memorized the data and shut the monitor off. Then he hurried across the room. One wall was covered by a long curtain. Boba grabbed the curtain and yanked it back.

Crimson sunset light flooded the chamber. A floor-to-ceiling shuttered window looked down onto the gleaming towers and chasms of Galactic City.

"Nice view," said Boba. "Hate to ruin it, but —"

His booted foot smashed through the transparent material. Cool air flowed inside, along with the sounds of the night city — airspeeders, distant voices. Boba stepped to the very edge of the sill. He looked down, adjusting his helmet for night vision.

"There it is," he said.

In the distance, he could see the immense dome of the Senate Building shining in the twilight. Boba tensed. Wind rushed past him through the shattered window. Somewhere in the Jedi Temple, someone would be looking for the mysterious envoy in Mandalorian armor.

No one could find him here.

Boba stared at the vast expanse of Galactic City, its lowest depths more than a kilometer below him.

He took a step forward.

He jumped.

For a second he was in free fall. Then his jet pack roared to life. Boba angled the controls so that he flew swiftly from the Jedi Temple. Seconds later it was safely behind him, hidden by other towering skyscrapers.

He flew toward the Senate. If anyone had wanted to, they could have looked up and seen him — a tall figure in dark-green body armor, his head hidden by a Mandalorian battle helmet.

But no one knew to look for Boba Fett. He flew swiftly and unseen through the great city's high rise canyons, past shining buildings and domes, past bright clubs teeming with nightlife. He saw airspeeders and swoop bikes, air limos, taxis, freighters. Once he even thought he glimpsed Elan's bright-red speeder, darting down to the lowest levels of the city.

But Boba had no time for any of that now. He had only one thought in mind: Find Mace and destroy him. Even meeting with Palpatine paled beside that.

Nothing was going to keep Boba Fett from his destination.

Nothing was going to keep him from his destiny.

The map he'd seen in Windu's room had shown that the Supreme Cancellor's official chambers were on the northeast side of the dome. As Boba drew nearer, he could see lights shining from the dome's upper windows. Inside, figures moved.

The Senators. Palpatine wouldn't be with them, though. He'd be preparing for his meeting with Mace Windu — and then his meeting with Boba Fett.

"Palpatine's expecting me, but not this soon," Boba muttered as his jet pack brought him closer to the building. "And I doubt he's expecting me to land on his windowsill!"

But Boba had no desire to confront Palpatine's security guards. And Boba especially didn't want Mace Windu to have the advantage of seeing him first. He powered down his jet pack, aiming for a wide ledge two levels above Palpatine's chambers.

In a moment he landed smoothly on the ledge. A quick look around reassured him that he'd gone undetected.

"Made it!" he exclaimed.

He grabbed the rappelling line on his utility belt and stooped. He fastened the hook to the ledge, yanking at it to test that it would hold. Then he slowly let himself down, his gloved hands tight around the rope.

This was the risky part. If someone happened to pass by inside, Boba would be seen.

And that wouldn't be good. At best, he'd be detained and questioned before being released to Palpatine.

At worst —

That's not gonna happen!

Boba pushed the thought away.

Down, down, down. He braced himself against the dome's wall. The dome was curved and smooth. Sometimes his boots slid off, despite their magnatomic soles.

Uh-oh!

In his hands, the rope suddenly grew slack. Boba looked up and saw the hook wobbling slightly.

Gotta hurry!

He was level with Palpatine's chamber now. There was no one there — no one he could see, anyway.

It was now or never!

He kicked out, swinging back, then forward. His boots grazed the ledge. He kicked again, propelling himself farther back. Then he began to swoop in toward the ledge again.

Oh no!

A twist of rope looped around his hands. Boba looked up quickly.

Two levels above him, the grappling hook tore away. The rope began to fall.

But Boba's feet had already found purchase on the ledge outside Palpatine's chamber. For an instant he swayed, perilously close to plunging off.

Then he caught his balance.

That was close!

Boba straightened. In front of him, black transparisteel showed his reflection. He replaced the rappelling line and withdrew a small laser blade. Its ruby tip glowed as he began to cut a hole in the window, just big enough for his hand to pass through. When the hole was completed, he carefully removed the transparisteel. He slid his hand inside, expertly finding the alarm system, then disabling it. His hand slipped down and pulled the latch.

The window swung open.

He was in!

Now to find Mace . . .

The room was small and dim. It smelled faintly of expensive spices. Thick carpet was underfoot, and small lights cast a soft glow over a door and sculptures at one end.

That's the antechamber, he thought. *That's where Mace is.*

Silently he stepped to the door. He put his hand on the latch. It was unlocked. He listened, adjusting his helmet's aural enhancers so he could hear the faintest sound from the other side.

And yes, he could hear breathing. The breathing was slow, measured, calm . . .

Boba drew his flechette pistol. He took a deep breath then shoved the door open.

And there he was. Boba's greatest enemy —

Mace Windu.

CHAPTER SEVENTEEN

The tall Jedi stood pensively at the far end of the room. His hands were in his robes. His head was down. As Boba entered he looked up, eyes widening slightly.

"Who —?"

Boba stared at him without remorse.

"You killed my father," he said.

Boba's heart was racing. But his voice was cold and utterly calm.

And his pistol was aimed directly at Mace's chest.

"I've waited a long time for this, Jedi Windu — but I'm not waiting anymore!"

Boba fired. The flechette's missile tore through the air. A nanosecond later it burst open. Hundreds of deadly projectiles spun out.

Faster than thought, Mace Windu leaped aside. The missiles exploded against the wall.

"Who are you?" Mace Windu shouted.

Boba fired again. Another starburst of flechettes exploded through the room.

Again, the Jedi was too fast.

"On Geonosis, you murdered a warrior named Jango Fett," Boba said.

FFFFAAMM! He fired again!

"Jango Fett was my father."

"Your father?" Mace raced from the barrage of flechettes. "He had no son! Only clones —"

"He had me!" Boba lunged at Mace. The Jedi fell back, overwhelmed by the young man's rage and power. "And now I'll have you!"

KRACK!

A flechette smashed against Mace's shoulder. The Jedi reeled backward. His hand reached for his lightsaber. But before he could touch it Boba struck again, this time the other shoulder. And again!

KRACK! KRACK!

With each alternate blow the Jedi fell back. In a moment, Boba would have him pinioned against the wall. And then — he'd go for the kill!

"I had no choice!" Mace's voice was deep, unafraid. Without warning he leaped, springing past Boba as he drew his lightsaber. "Just as you're giving me no choice now!"

The lightsaber glowed deep violet. Its hum filled the room, and Mace Windu swung — and struck!

FAM!

Boba staggered back. The lightsaber had skimmed his armor. He recovered immediately, darting off. Mace followed, his robes billowing behind him.

FAM!

The lightsaber struck again!

But this time Boba was ready. Or so he thought. Mace's violet blur sliced the flechette pistol cleanly out of his hand. Blinding indigo light flared as Mace Windu drew back, arm raised for another blow.

Before he could strike, Boba drew his dagger with his free hand and charged.

The dagger ripped through Mace's robes. The Jedi twisted, avoiding the blade.

But Boba's fist followed, smashing into the Jedi's ribs.

"Ah —!"

Mace staggered to one side. Before he could dodge, Boba was on him!

BAM!

Boba lunged the dagger at Mace's head — but the Jedi was too fast! He dropped and rolled, jumping to his feet. The lightsaber rose and fell —

And struck.

"Agh!" Boba cried out as the glowing blade smashed against his shoulder. Pain arced through him. Blood seeped from Grievous's wound.

"Surrender!" commanded Mace Windu. "Surrender, and I promise you'll receive fair treatment!"

"Surrender?" Boba hesitated, feigning doubt. Unseen he shoved the dagger into his belt, then reached for a cryo-ban grenade.

"You have my word," Mace continued.

"And you have my hatred!" Boba screamed.

He fired the grenade!

Mace leaped, seeming to fly above Boba's head.

BRRAAANG!

Boba flung himself away from the freezing blast. Waves of numbing cold rushed past him as the cryo-blast absorbed heat. The cold could not penetrate Boba's body armor. . . .

But Mace Windu had no body armor. The Jedi stumbled, nearly falling as the frigid waves sapped him of energy. Boba picked up his flechette pistol. He towered above the fallen Jedi.

He fired.

FAM!

Blinding pain lanced Boba's arm as Mace Windu's lightsaber struck.

"No!" Boba cried.

In agony, Boba fell. He rolled, trying to get to his feet.

FAM!

The lightsaber crashed against his head. Not even his helmet could absorb the blow. Boba shouted with pain and fury, striking blindly at the figure above him.

"I don't want to kill you," said Mace Windu grimly. "Surrender, or die."

"Never."

He swung his dagger. The Jedi's weapon knocked the dagger blade aside.

"You leave me no choice!" Mace cried.

Boba stumbled to his feet. Blood streamed from his wounds. The dagger lay useless and out of reach. And his blasters were on *Slave I*.

But he still had the saberdart. He slid his hand toward his utility belt. His fingers slipped into the familiar configuration of his palm shooter. The poisonous dart was loaded into it.

He had only one shot.

I won't miss this time.

He raised his hand. Mace Windu was just meters away. Boba stared at the Jedi, summoning all his strength. All his hatred.

His thumb pressed the trigger.

The dart sang from the palm shooter like an enraged hornet. It spun, glittering, through the air, straight for Mace Windu's throat.

I got him! Boba's mind sang in triumph.

Mace Windu flinched. His hand shot into the air. Between his fingers the saberdart shivered like a trapped insect.

"No!" groaned Boba.

Mace Windu flung the deadly dart into the shadows. He stepped toward Boba, his lightsaber poised to strike.

Boba Fett was cornered.

"This is my final offer of surrender," said the Jedi Master.

"No," said Boba in a low voice.

He would never surrender.

The Jedi took another step toward him. Boba thought of his friends back on Tatooine.

Good-bye, Ygabba. Good-bye, Gab'borah. I'll miss you.

He thought of his father, fighting until the very

last. Boba lifted his head and stared fearlessly at Mace Windu.

"There are worse things than death," the bounty hunter said, raising his flechette pistol.

"There are," the Jedi replied in his powerful voice. "You are brave indeed, stranger. I would have spared your life. But now you leave me no choice —"

His raised his arms. The glowing light blade tore through the air.

"STOP!"

A deafening shout of command filled the room. Heavy footsteps echoed as uniformed guards raced in. The Chancellor's Red Guards surrounded Mace Windu and Boba.

More footsteps sounded. Another figure entered the room, clad in the luxurious robes denoting his high rank.

"Who dares disrupt this place?" he demanded.

It was Supreme Chancellor Palpatine.

CHAPTER EIGHTEEN

"Your Eminence," said Mace Windu. He deactivated his lightsaber and took a respectful step back. "I arrived a few minutes early for our meeting, and found this intruder in your antechamber."

He gestured at Boba. Palpatine turned. He stared at the bounty hunter. The Supreme Chancellor nodded at Boba, almost imperceptibly.

"This man is not a stranger to me," said Palpatine. "I was expecting him."

"Expecting him!" Windu exclaimed. "But —"

Palpatine turned to calmly face the Jedi. No longer was Palpatine the soft-spoken, thoughtful figure who had first come to prominence in the Senate. Now the Chancellor radiated power — and arrogance.

"Do you *dare* question me?" he asked. "This bounty hunter has important *information* — information vital to the Republic! And will your bickering interfere with him bringing it to us?"

For a moment the Jedi said nothing. Then he nodded.

"I was unaware of your meeting. My sole concern was for your safety and the safety of the Republic."

Palpatine waved a hand toward the Red Guards. "As you can see, I am not unprotected. I am, as always, grateful for your support. But now, Master Windu, you may leave."

Palpatine inclined his head toward the door. Boba blinked. He swiftly replaced his weapons, and waited.

Mace Windu bowed slightly. But his eyes were on Boba. "Yes, your Eminence. The Jedi Council will question this bounty hunter after his meeting with you —"

"Perhaps."

Mace Windu walked to the door. At the last moment he paused and looked back at Boba. A long, hard look. Then the door closed behind him. Boba was alone with Supreme Chancellor Palpatine.

"I seem to be having a problem with people arriving early for their meetings," the Chancellor said smoothly.

He looked at Boba and smiled, but there was no warmth in his eyes.

Boba nodded. "I regret the inconvenience," he said.

He took a step forward, wincing at the pain. The Chancellor gestured at Boba's helmet.

"You may remove that," he said in his calmly ominous voice. "I know who you are — Boba Fett."

Boba sucked his breath in sharply. Then he did as the Chancellor had commanded, and held the helmet at his side.

"I know you are the Hutt clan's foremost bounty hunter," Palpatine went on. "I also know that you yourself are being hunted — by Count Dooku. And by Durge."

"I don't deny it," Boba replied.

"You say you have news for me. Information." Palpatine's eyes glittered. His hands smoothed the folds of his rich, long robes. "I am waiting."

Boba glanced at the Red Guards, and Palpatine motioned for Boba to follow him into his office. Once they were alone, Boba spoke.

"You are at war against the Separatists," said Boba. "Count Dooku leads the Separatist cause. He is your most dangerous enemy and has vast droid armies. You have gathered a powerful force of clones. These clones were created by someone named Tyranus. Tyranus is your ally — or so you think.

"But I know the truth, Chancellor."

Boba stopped.

The time had come for him to reveal what he knew. The secret had given him strength and purpose for years. He would reveal it now, to the Supreme Chancellor.

By aligning himself with Palpatine, Boba would gain more strength. He would be well paid for his information. Then he could leave and return to Tatooine in triumph, even though Wat Tambor had eluded him.

"I am waiting," said Palpatine in a low voice.

"I learned of this when I was a prisoner of the Count on Raxus Prime. I was a boy then. He thought he had no need to fear me. But he was wrong."

Boba took a breath. Then he said, "Count Dooku and Tyranus are the same person. Your greatest enemy created your armies. It is a trap."

Palpatine lifted his head. His greedy, deepset eyes gleamed with avarice and the joy of knowledge. The joy of power.

The joy of triumph.

"I know," he said.

CHAPTER NINETEEN

Boba hesitated. "You . . . already know?"

Palpatine nodded. His hands slipped inside the folds of his robes.

"There is nothing I do not know," he said. "Nothing that is worth knowing, anyway."

"But — but why —"

Palpatine's hand shot out, ordering silence. "That information is not yours to command, Boba Fett. It is mine alone."

Palpatine looked closely at Boba, then continued. "I have heard much of your prowess as a tracker and bounty hunter. I know how your father died. I know who killed him — and why. When you arrived here I knew you would hunt down that Jedi Master."

Boba stood, stunned.

"I have already arranged for your ship to be brought here from the Jedi Temple," said Palpatine.

"You will be escorted to it in a few moments. You will leave Coruscant immediately. And you will say nothing of this meeting to anyone — ever."

Palpatine withdrew his hand from his robe. He held it out to Boba. A shining credit cube glittered in his palm.

"This should be ample compensation for you, bounty hunter. I believe we have an agreement and I believe we share a common enemy."

Palpatine's mouth curved in a small, sinister smile. Boba looked at him, then at the credit cube. He took the cube, then nodded.

"I will never say a word," Boba replied.

"You had better not," said Palpatine calmly. From the hallway echoed the sound of the Red Guards.

Boba pulled his helmet back over his head. He grimaced, but he could live with the pain. He could live with returning to Tatooine.

He could live with a lot of things, with the fortune Palpatine had given him.

CHAPTER TWENTY

Slave I shot into the velvety sky above Coruscant. Far, far below, the spectral lights of Galactic City shimmered and glowed, then began to grow fainter and fainter as Boba's ship hurtled off. In a few moments, Coruscant was only a glittering speck in all the galaxy.

And soon, even Coruscant had disappeared.

Behind the controls, Boba Fett sat pensively. He'd already arranged for Palpatine's credits to be stashed in an account on Aargau. That way, Boba could access them whenever he needed them. And no one else could — not even Jabba.

The Huttese gangster might question Boba returning without Wat Tambor. But as the battle between the Republic and the Separatists continued to rage, Boba suspected that Jabba would find other things to occupy his greedy little mind.

Besides, Boba was no longer intimidated by the

thought of Jabba the Hutt. Boba had enough credits to last him the rest of his life. He could pick and choose his bounties, selecting only the ones that challenged him.

And there would be plenty of those! He'd already heard rumors of a kidnapping on Rodia. But first he might take a little time off and amuse himself. The All-Human Free-For-All on Jubilar would be held soon. He might go to that. He could use a break. . . .

The past was behind Boba now. His father was long buried. Boba had not killed Mace Windu, but he suspected that great troubles awaited him — and all Jedi. And the love and respect Jango had felt for his son would not die. And Boba's love for his father would not change, either.

Mace Windu had been a powerful opponent. And a worthy one. But there would be many more. Boba Fett knew that. He leaned forward, staring out at the vastness of space.

It was a big place, the galaxy. Endless, dangerous, exciting. A million adventures waited out there, for anyone bold enough to take them.

Boba's course was set. He had a ship full of weapons, and Slave I was the best ship in the galaxy.

Boba smiled. The future was his.

And he was on his way to seize it.